THE SAFFRON COLLECTORS

BEAUTIFUL TRAITOR BOOKS

THE SAFFRON COLLECTORS

A World where Transformation is Contagious

KINGSLEY L. DENNIS

Illustrated by
Naomi Hasegawa

Published by Beautiful Traitor Books –
http://www.beautifultraitorbooks.com/

ISBN-13: 978-1-9999053-2-3   (paperback)

First published: 2018

Cover Image & Internal Drawings: Naomi Hasegawa
Front Cover & Book Design – Ibolya Kapta

Acknowledgements: The author would like to express his deep gratitude and thanks to Naomi Hasegawa and Ibolya Kapta. Naomi's wonderful illustrations have made this book come alive. Her gift has been a generous one, and her gentle presence pervades these pages. And Ibolya has been a saffron collector from the beginning.

DEDICATION

For those who are interested in what the saffron
has to teach us

*If the outer sun rises but the inner sun does
not, then nothing has been gained*

La Madre

TERESA

The universe is not the expression of mathematical equations – it is the play of poetic forces; and like a child it is intoxicated with love and wonder, and the joyful curiosity of adventure.

CHAPTER ONE

~ Only those who take the first step can learn to walk ~

The little girl stepped quietly into the room, not wishing to make a sound. Not wishing to disturb the speckles of dust drifting through the rays of the sun. The morning light had risen early, as it did during the summer days. The heat was also beginning to rise up, getting ready to infiltrate through the slightly parted window. The tiniest of breezes brought in a whisper of scent as the last traces of jasmine, the lady of the night, crept in. The little girl stood still, waiting patiently. Her senses stilled to the unspoken rhythm of the room. She counted her breaths as each one rose and fell; as if each breath was her companion. Her eyes lighted upon the figure seated near the window.

Teresa was five years old. Entering the room of La Madre was one of her earliest, most definable memories. It was in that moment – in that guarded slice of space and time – that everything began. Everything remembered previously had slipped away the instant Teresa had stepped into the room. She would always recollect that sun- glazed morning as the first day of her life. That was the first time she had ever met La Madre, and first meetings never come again no matter how hard you wish for them. They are precious, like a jewelled kiss.

CHAPTER TWO

*~ Not everyone who arrives will stay. Not everyone
who stays has arrived ~*

The girls all awoke in the hour after sunrise and dressed to eat in the communal dining hall. The elder girls would soon leave for the morning picking, whilst the younger ones would stay and help to clear up. Teresa was expected to learn fast the ways of the orphanage. These were some of the things in which she had no choice; like having no choice in being singled out for the new program at the Azafran Home for Girls. They accepted only a very few young girls each year, yet according to what criteria Teresa could never guess. Teresa had arrived tired, confused, and with little need beyond adequate shelter and some decent care.

A state carer had brought Teresa by car to the front of the large house, situated at the end of a long gravel track. Teresa had sat silently in the back of the car as the hills passed by as if on a long colourful reel. She remembered trying to decide if the countryside looked welcoming, harsh, or indifferent. She always liked to guess silently within her the nature of things. On the day of her arrival she had looked out at the landscape, and asked herself if the trees leaning in the fields approved of her passing – or did they consider it a trespass upon their terrain? *I'm just passing through, dear fields* – Teresa had mouthed the words silently as if etching air. *Do you know where they are taking me?* she had asked.

With her head pressed against the pane of the passenger window, with closed eyes, the car had delivered their new child. So many things had happened to Teresa in so few years that she hadn't had time to know what things were permanent in her life. Her little soul felt as if it had relinquished control of any direction, and her body was a seed in the wind. She had not the words to articulate this; but it was how she felt inside on the day she arrived. And it was inside where Teresa preferred to live, where the butterflies swam and the bees burrowed by.

The house had looked like a mansion to Teresa. No, it looked more like a monastery; somewhere full of praying people and big rooms full of silence and stone. Despite the enormity of the building Teresa had felt a welcoming nature to it. Maybe, she thought, it had opened an invisible portal only for her to approach and enter. Everybody else would be turned away, not accepted by the spirit of the stones. Teresa's mind had sped in circles as the car came to a halt and the engine ceased. It was another place, another step, for Teresa's tiniest of feet. As soon as the passenger door of the car had been opened Teresa hopped out. She hadn't wanted to delay any further.

That day was now gone, severed from its past. And yet, like many events at the orphanage, it had been collected into the present, along with her other belongings of mind, memory, and feelings.

The day after her arrival Teresa had been taken to see La Madre, the matriarch of the orphanage. It had been an exceptionally warm morning.

CHAPTER THREE

~ Nothing in this world is without its rhyme or reason ~

Teresa approached as the seated figure beckoned to her. She had been told to be respectful and courteous; for it was with La Madre's blessing that she was being cared for. Teresa, walking softly in her slippers, felt the stone floor flatly press against the soles of her feet. The floor was cool, and gave off a smell of antiquity and assurance. Teresa stopped walking as she approached to the side of the large wooden chair. She observed La Madre's side profile as the older lady continued to gaze out of the half-shuttered window. A ray of light fell across her shoulder, and made Teresa think of a princess's shawl. When La Madre turned her head Teresa was greeted with a warm smile.

'Welcome, Teresa. You walk so carefully I could hardly hear you come in.'

Teresa felt a small blush arise upon her cheeks. She looked down, not wishing to show it.

'Give me your hands, Teresa.' Teresa stepped forward and let La Madre take her hands. As the elder lady looked closely at the young girl's hands, turning them over and feeling the softness of their palms, Teresa was inspecting the face of her new patron. The lady was not as old as Teresa had thought. Her face still had some of its youngish features, and her skin looked smooth, not yet beset by wrinkles or other touches of time. There was a stillness in La Madre's features that matched the tranquillity of the room and the strength of its stone. Teresa gave out a long breath and relaxed as her hands were gently returned to her, and fell by her sides in rest.

'Do you know what we do here, Teresa?'

Teresa shook her head.

'We gather and collect things - but not for ourselves. We are not keepers. We collect in order to give away. Do you understand what that means?'

Teresa nodded her head. La Madre smiled and reached out to stroke the little girl's cheek.

'Unlike many of the others in the world, what we do here is not for ourselves. But in doing so, we also help ourselves. This is how *we* understand the world.'

Teresa gave out a very soft 'Yesss' and her s's slipped from her tongue like a trail of feathers.

'Good. We shall be very happy to have you amongst us, Teresa.'

La Madre reached over and planted a soft kiss upon Teresa's forehead. It was a tender touch of affection that Teresa was not accustomed to. A warm tingling energy went through her body and seemed to pour out from the top of her head. That was the first day Teresa remembered feeling truly alive. And it was the first of many.

CHAPTER FOUR

~ A generous heart always seeks to re-establish harmony ~

Teresa helped clear up the breakfast tables along with some of the other younger girls. There were smiles and glances amongst them although their solidarity was quiet and non-intrusive. It seemed to Teresa that the sounds of the stone building were more important than the sounds of chattering mouths. Useless talk did not arise amongst those within its walls, and Teresa felt grateful for this. In her previous homes she had wanted to hide herself away from the other girls because they talked too loudly and acted too brash. Teresa had become withdrawn; and in her withdrawal she had become visible to others. Seemingly out of the blue a request for her attendance had been issued by the Azafran Foundation. This had led to the proceedings that finally delivered her to the orphanage of stone buildings covered in creeping vines and jasmine, known as the Azafran Home for Girls.

Until the girls were older they were not permitted to enter the fields, yet Teresa was desperate to go.

'Why don't they let us go?'

The other young girl looked over at Teresa and shrugged. Her name was Alicia and she was seven years old.

'When we're older we can go picking.'

'Picking? What do we pick?'

'The flowers, of course. They all pick flowers here.'

Teresa smiled. That sounded like a good idea to her. 'Can we not pick before?'

Alicia shrugged again, then grinned. 'Why don't you ask La Madre?'

'Maybe I will.' The idea entered into her mind and took its place amidst the rest of Teresa's wandering thoughts. Only that this thought wanted to give itself more importance, and so it sat higher in her mind, closer to the top of her skull where she could not ignore it.

The young girls liked to play, especially outside now that the summer days were sprinkling the stone orphanage with patches of heat. There were squares, triangles, and also other more unusual shapes of sun patches that played against the shadows along the outer nooks and corners of the buildings. It was like a tapestry of heat and shade, of light and shadow, which wove an interplay of contrasts from morning until the evenings. In the playground of the orphanage the girls played and invented their games – they skipped, clapped, sang, and danced like all young girls have done at some moment in their lives. These were the joyful, unobtrusive moments where life is like an older girl that takes your hand and guides you into play. In such moments life hides the veils of sorrow; of scars and of suffering. These guiding hands were decorated with unusual ink designs that showed strange animals, flowers, and a wide world of possibilities. Teresa, like the other young girls, took these hands and allowed them to be their guides through the many days of work and play.

Each afternoon a class of gymnastics was held for the girls. Yet these classes were not comprised of the usual rolling and running, but rather a series of postures and stretches. Anna, an older girl of sixteen, was the teacher of the classes. Her lengthy blonde hair was tied into a pony-tail, and her face was thin and sleek. Teresa watched her carefully, her own big brown eyes taking in each detail as if it was a piece to a puzzle. Anna's manner was calm, and her movements, thought Teresa, were as if swimming through air. Teresa admired Anna for she was unlike the other girls she had come across before. It was only later, when Teresa had learned the word graceful, that she knew what she wanted to say to describe her. And then soon after that she learned the word harmonious, and that became another Anna word. Teresa was excited with each new pairing, how she could match up new words with their person. It allowed her to see the world in action; it was when words could be given to things that life became more practical. It was then that things seemed to fit more.

'Why are we twisting our bodies like this, Anna?'
All the other girls looked at Teresa. No one else had dared to ask such direct questions before. Anna walked over to where Teresa was seated and placed both hands upon her back and gently pushed to lower her body further to the floor.
'That's better,' said Anna as she walked back to the front of the class. 'We do this twisting because it's good for our bodies, and our minds. We call it a kind of yoga.'
Some of the younger girls giggled.
'Yogi, yoda, yogurt…' they whispered and giggled. Teresa too giggled quietly but did not say anything.
Anna clasped her hands together and pressed them against

her smiling lips.

'Yes, it's an unusual name. But whatever it's called – yoga or yoghurt,' and here some of the girls giggled again, 'it will help to balance you.' Anna spoke with a soft and calm voice. Teresa traced Anna's words in the air as they spiralled out of her mouth and somersaulted, like yoga letters.

Teresa tried harder to bend her body into the new postures. Her mind willed her body as if they were friends coming together.

Teresa noticed also that Anna was observing her.

CHAPTER FIVE

~ Ignorance is not cured by adopting the easiest methods ~

On Tuesday and Thursday afternoons La Madre would come to the playground to talk to the young girls. For many of them this was a highlight in their week. They all loved and respected La Madre and wished that she would spend more time amongst them. Yet La Madre had many duties to perform, and a lot of her time was also spent with the older girls. So those Tuesday and Thursday moments were precious for the younger girls and for Teresa too.

By late Tuesday afternoon the playground was in shade. A warm shade that sheltered the skin from the burning kisses of the sun. All the girls took their gymnastic exercise mats and placed them on the floor in front of the big chair. They sat, and shifted and shuffled their small bodies. Only when La Madre appeared did they cease their restlessness and sit to attention. La Madre walked in dressed in a long, flowing dress of white linen that Teresa thought covered her entire body like a bed sheet. The older lady's dark hair trickled down the side of her face and curved behind her ears before falling gently across her shoulders. La Madre lowered herself slowly upon the chair and placed her hands upon her lap. Her every movement was precise and smooth. Teresa told herself quietly in her own mind that La Madre had no jagged edges. Her skin too was darker than Teresa had first thought. Maybe La Madre had herself been out in the fields under the sun picking her own flowers. It was a face darkened by the heated touch of the sun, and yet polished by the brushing of flowers against it. Teresa imagined La Madre bent over a bright pink flower, putting her nose into its pinky petals and inhaling the colour into her own skin. It was only later, when Teresa knew more words, that she thought back at this image and re-named it a flower transfusion. Maybe there were aspects of nature, she thought, that could be transfused into human bodies like a type of food.

La Madre looked out across the group of young girls and

a wide smile spread across her face.

'Education is one of the reasons why we are here.' When she spoke it was in a firm voice that could have been a mixture of mahogany wood with ancient stone. 'If we do not educate ourselves, we cannot be educated for the world. We all arrive here as little ones, dependent and incomplete. We must earn our independence, and work towards our completion. Does this make some sense to you?'

All the young girls nodded their heads, as if a breeze had passed through their hair and made a sea of browns and yellows. La Madre gave a slight smile and pressed her hands together.

'You are all young, and there is much to learn. The good news is that learning never stops – it is like a river that flows endlessly. I myself am still learning, still swimming in that flowing river. It shall take us through our whole life, accompanying us through all our years. Yet here, we wish to allow you a different type of education. Learning is not about four walls and examinations.'

La Madre paused and scanned the enthusiastic young faces. Then her gaze dropped lightly upon Teresa, and for a short instant there was a line of connection. And then La Madre broke away and moved on, and Teresa could not be sure if she had imagined the momentary halt, or whether it was a flicker in time, like when a movie fleetingly jars.

'For us here, education is not a certificate or a diploma. It is not a static piece of paper that one puts away to gather dust. Education is ongoing and continual, and it must be alive, like the fruit that hangs from the tree, or the flowers that bend in the breeze. And like all living things, it contains within it the inner longing to understand more – to grow in mindfulness, gratitude, and appreciation. Education is a world that opens up within and inspires you to go forth with a great energy, trust, and with the incalculable sense of wonder. Everything is a wonder – is it not?'

A *yess* rippled through the group, coupled with the warmth of the shade that made Teresa feel as if embraced, cuddled, by a loving giant hand. Maybe there was more to the world than she had been told. Perhaps there had been a reason for her silence, her retreat, in the years before. Maybe she was not alone.

Alicia, who was next to Teresa, nudged her and when she turned she saw a cheeky smile upon her friend's face.
'Why so serious?' whispered Alicia.
Teresa giggled back, showing that she had snapped out of her brief reverie.

La Madre held up her hand and picked up the strings of silence.

'And there's a reason also why we all do the gymnastics. I know all this body stretching may seem a little odd to some of you girls. What we do here is not often done elsewhere. In this place, the body matters as well as the mind. Education also involves the body – to prepare it for a different type of environment, where different energies and impacts are active. We also should have discipline over the body, and to listen to it. When we listen to our bodies we are listening also to our larger mind. The mind is not only in the head,' and La Madre brought her right hand to her forehead, 'but is in the whole body. It listens to us – did you know that?'

Later that evening after supper the girls were all lying quietly in their beds. Scented candles were always lit in the evenings, in little ceramic bowls that cast intricate shadows across the walls. Shadow shapes like animal souls danced along the painted stone as if enacting their histories. Some of the girls would lie wide-eyed awake watching the shapes flicker and shift. Whispers like wind grazing flowers floated over across the beds. It felt cosy to Teresa, who that night was sunk into her bed like it was her cocoon. She had felt this cosiness from the first night she had slept at the orphanage. It had engulfed her warmly as if covered by a bed of earth.

'Psss…'

Teresa turned her head to the side, her bed sheet pulled up almost to her ears.

'Hey, Teresa?' It was her bed neighbour, a girl of the same age who was called Tibia.

'Yes?'

'Are you listening to your body?' Tibia giggled and pushed her head into her pillow.

Teresa giggled back. 'I'm trying to!'

'What's it saying?'

'That it wants less gymnastics…'

Both girls giggled quietly, and added hushed tones to the low vibratory chatter of the room.

'Hey, Tibia?'

'Yeah?'

'I'm glad there are no exams here. I don't like that kind of learning,' said Teresa softly.

'Me too…'

Then after a short pause, Teresa said 'Our minds must be really big…'

'Why?' asked Tibia sleepily.

'Well, if the mind is in the whole body, like La Madre says it is, then we have it everywhere, don't we?'

'Mmm,' replied a drowsy Tibia, 'suppose so.'

'And then it's in our heart – and in our fingers and toes too. We must really be much bigger than we think…or maybe it's thinking bigger than we are…'

Tibia yawned and rolled over, pushing her head further into the pillow.

And the soul of a cat sprinted up from the candle flame and caught the leg of a fleeting bird. Teresa pushed her head down and watched the play, until her eyes grew heavy. Sleep soon came to visit, and tucked Teresa's own soul into bed before jumping inside to listen to her body, and her whole mind.

CHAPTER SIX

~ Supreme self-discipline is the same as sincere surrender ~

After breakfast Teresa and the other girls of her age helped to clear up the dishes and take them to the kitchens to be washed. The older women who ran the orphanage, who were known as the Madams, spoke little and yet moved in a way as if each one knew what they were doing. It fascinated Teresa to watch them. Now and again they would give the younger girls a directive, a job to do, and they would speak quietly and yet firmly, and almost always with a smile. None of the girls disobeyed or argued, least of all the older girls who were in their adolescent years. Things just seemed to get done. And whilst Teresa knew that certain things had to be done, she felt the urge to test this – to know why.

One of the older Madams, known as Pym, was head of the kitchens. Her greying hair was neatly tucked behind her ears and her small rounded face, with its few curvy wrinkles, seemed to gleam like an orb. She had motioned for Teresa to come over to her.

'Yes, Madam Pym?'

'Teresa, please find our Madam Celia, and tell her from me that I would like her stock papers.'

Teresa paused. Her mind shifted quickly through the information. She knew who Madam Celia was; she was the red-haired lady who was in charge of buying everything for the orphanage. She was known to be very efficient, and extremely sharp-eyed. The girls liked her because she said funny things from time to time, and made jokes about the place. But why? Why was she being asked to do this errand… it was a simple question that Teresa had lingering upon her tongue.

Madam Pym noticed the slight hesitancy in Teresa's behaviour.

'Teresa, did you understand what I said?'

Teresa nodded. 'Yes, Madam Pym. I understood what you said. But why?'

'Why what?' Madam Pym raised a questioning eyebrow.

'Why do I need to do it?'

'So you will not do it?'

'If you tell me why, I will.' Teresa's tone had slipped out of her mouth more defiant than she had wanted. She didn't want to be defiant, she only wished to know why. It was just a simple question.

Madam Pym looked straight into Teresa's eyes and said one word in a firm, low voice. 'Discipline.'

The encounter happened suddenly, as if it had just popped up from the floor, like those figures that pop-up in some children's story books when you open them. They kind of spring at you, and you just wish to look at them whilst ignoring the text. That's somehow like Teresa felt when she ran into La Madre in one of the corridors that led in from the outside yard. Teresa's eyes had not had time to fully adjust back to the shaded light of the interior. She almost knocked into the figure dressed in white, which to Teresa's eyes was still a grey blur.

'Sorry Madam, I didn't…oh, La Madre!' Teresa felt herself blushing and tried to hide her face away. 'Sorry, I didn't see you,' she said in a soft voice of embarrassment and shame.

'It's Teresa, isn't it?' La Madre's voice was calm, and sounded as if it could have come from the shadows, or from the silence itself. They were words absent of noise.

Teresa nodded. 'Yes, La Madre.'

'And do you know *why* your name is Teresa?'

There was a short pause. 'Because my parents gave that name to me.'

'My name is Teresa because my parents gave me that name,' repeated La Madre.

Teresa blushed. 'Yes. My name is Teresa because my parents gave me that name.'

'No, that is not why.'

A ripple of confusion appeared across Teresa's face.

'Your parents, or your guardians, may have given you your name – but that is not *why* you have the name you have. Your name is Teresa for a very special reason. It is so, and yet you may not know it. Until the time you are able to understand the *whys* and *wherefores* of this world you need to first understand obedience. Unless you are able to do a thing, you will not be able to understand the *why* of it. Do my words make sense to you, Teresa?'

Teresa nodded that she understood. La Madre smiled and bent her head lower so that she came closer to Teresa.

'And perhaps a curious girl such as yourself wants also to

know *why* she cannot go out in the mornings to pick flowers like the older girls?'

This time Teresa really did blush. She felt a new heat in the shadows of the corridor, as if the stone walls had begun to radiate out the warmth of the sun from outside. But the heat was not from without – it came from a place deep within Teresa's own small body.

La Madre placed her hand softly upon the girl's shoulder.

'For now, my little Teresa, I'm going to ask some of the other girls to pick flowers for you – so that you can learn something new. A new game!'

La Madre let out a little, low laugh that mingled into Teresa's hair and tingled. And then she was gone.

CHAPTER SEVEN

~ The absence of noise is a negative silence – a positive
silence is different ~

There were several white clouds hugging together in the sky, muffling the sounds of flocking birds. Teresa and Tibia were hugging against the walls of the stone orphanage as they crept around the building trying to stay in the shadow. It was shortly after breakfast, after they had finished their clearing duties, and now the young girls were exploring. The orphanage was still a large place for them, with nooks and crannies of stone that held back from the telling of their stories. Stone speaks little, preferring a silence that absorbs and stores rather than fleets away. At the back of the orphanage stood a large well that bored down deep into the earth and her water below. The two young girls now peered over the edge of this circular wall of stone, clasping at the side and heaving their bodies up. A dank, moist, and yet cool field of air sank into their nostrils and enveloped their faces. An unknown darkness reached up from below, and for Teresa it almost felt as if it was eerily beckoning to them.

Tibia shivered. 'Ergh, I don't like it. It's so far down. Anything could be there.'

'Things more than water?'

'Yes – lots more!'

'What's more than water down there?' Teresa's nose twitched, as if trying to fathom the smell of that unknown something more than water.

'Don't know. Don't wanna know. Maybe it's a big fish-snake kind of thing. Those kinds that eat you.'

Teresa paused for a few seconds. 'Are you scared?'

'I'm not scared, I'm just...' Tibia trailed off into a negative silence.

'No need to be scared – we're protected here.'

'We shouldn't even be here. It's not for us out back here. It's only for the older girls.'

'We'll be older one day,' replied Teresa quietly, as if caught up in a breeze of her own thoughts. 'And big fish-snakes don't bother me.'

'What does bother you then?'

Teresa sank back down from the well wall, brushed off her

dress and shrugged. 'Not knowing.'

'What?'

'That's what bothers me – not knowing.'

Tibia fell down beside Teresa and looked at her with a scrunched-up face.

Teresa grinned back at her with a cheeky look, before shouting 'Come!'

Teresa ran over the yard with Tibia following behind. The two young girls scampered along the side path that wound between an assortment of flowers planted on either side. They came to a large rectangular wooden fence perched between two large stone pillars. Teresa was the first to step onto the wooden slats of the fence and climb up. Resting her elbows on the top rung of the fence she gazed off into the distance. A warm hand of sunlight cradled her back as if supporting her.

'What do you see?' Tibia looked up from the base of the fence, her little fingers tapping against the wood.

'Fields, lots of fields. And lots of flowers too!'

'How many flowers? What colours?'

'More flowers than ever – and they're all colours! They're sprinkled all about like jelly beans. I want to go out there…'

'But you can't, you know that!'

'I don't know it!' But Teresa frowned, because she did.

The rest of the morning the two girls explored the perimeter of the orphanage, as if navigating their first voyage of discovery. Their legs were tired by the time it came for the afternoon gymnastics lesson, and this was noticed by their teacher Anna.

It was Thursday late afternoon, and the girls were seated in the playground waiting for La Madre to appear. A light breeze had carried in a sweet scent that visited the seated children and touched upon each one as it passed. Teresa was feeling a little tired, more so than usual. She glanced to her side and saw Tibia yawn, which made her feel a bit better knowing that she was not alone.

Soon the white flowing figure that was La Madre entered the playground and seated herself in the large chair. Teresa observed the wicker legs of the chair; how the wicker strands wound around and around, making a spiral that rose up to… Teresa caught La Madre's eye. She hadn't meant to, it was an accident – she had been looking at the chair legs. But it was too late, because in a sudden flash the image of Teresa and Tibia leaning over the stone well wall came up into her mind. So did the view of the fields and the flowers she had seen from on top of the gate. Teresa tried quickly to suppress these guilty images, yet they jumped up into her mind and she couldn't catch them. They were images scuttling away like salacious salamanders. Teresa came back to herself and saw that La Madre was already speaking on some subject. Perhaps they hadn't connected after all. It was just another bout of Teresa's over active imagination, and La Madre was not even looking in her direction. Her head was turned to the front and not to the side where Teresa was sitting.

Words filtered back into her mind and nudged at Teresa's sleepiness.

'It's all about you, my dears. It starts and stops with you – and this is something you must learn. It is something you should taste for yourself. The places you all came from are different. They do not see the world like we do, here at the Azafran Home for Girls.'

It was the first time Teresa had heard La Madre refer to the place with its official name. It sounded somewhat different coming from her tongue; from the odd yet soft lilt of her accent. It almost, thought Teresa, sounded what silver would be like if it was a language and not a metal thing. Then something seemed to snap inside her ear as if someone had clicked their finger and thumb so close, and suddenly she was alert for when the next words from La Madre arrived.

'In everything we do, we need to give our consent. We cannot go against our self. Discipline and obedience are strengtheners for our self, they are not tests or commands. They are the early foundations from which we learn something much stronger, more resilient, and something that stays with us forever. But first, we must give consent to ourselves. If we do not start with achieving little things, how will we ever move on to achieve the larger goals? We work on the little things first. And you should do this too, because you are little ones.' La Madre gave a warm smile and clasped her hands together. Her eyes seemed to sparkle in concert with the light of the lowering sun.

La Madre paused and gazed out over the collection of young, attentive faces before continuing. 'Like I said, everything that is done must be done with your consent. And it must come from within you – it is your sacred voice. Yet remember, the sacred is not only in the still, small voice that sings inside of you. It is also in all the voices, and all the silences, and all the spaces in-between. Search for it, and search well.'

Teresa's eyes widened in recognition, and her heart beat momentarily fast.

For the rest of that evening Teresa was unable to get out of her head the last two words that La Madre had spoken - *search well*. It was as if the words were toying with her, carving out the letters inside her little skull. Was this what La Madre meant when she said we should listen to our voice within? Teresa was unsure, and was struggling against a sense of the inevitable. There was something she could not avoid doing.

Later that evening, after supper in the great hall, Teresa had slipped out of the main building on the way to the bathrooms. She silently crept along the sides of the grand stone edifice toward where she knew she would find the stone well - *search well* repeated the strange voice in her head. The sun had dipped over the horizon and yet there remained a soft, hazy shimmering of orangey light across the sky. Teresa stepped lightly over to the well's circular stone wall and again pushed herself up to look over. She didn't know what to expect…a smell of musty water? A voice from far below? The sudden leap of a large fish-snake with a mouth of tiny, pointed teeth?

No, there was none of that. What she could see was a wire meshing that had been placed over the aperture of the well. Only tiny frogs perhaps could fall through such a small-

squared meshing; certainly no girls could. A jolt seized
Teresa as two hands fell upon her shoulders and eased her off
the wall. Teresa had not heard a sound, only the rasps of her
own heavy breathing. Yet she knew who it was – she
recognised the sweet scent.

La Madre's hands reached up from Teresa's shoulders
and into her long brown hair. The hands then brought all the
hair together and Teresa could feel one of the hands reaching
away for something. It returned, and her hair was tied back
into a pony-tail. Finally, with a light touch of indication from
the hands, Teresa turned around to face La Madre. She was
expecting a face of anger, or at least of disappointment. Yet
in its place was a calm face of curiosity and, thought Teresa,
maybe even a slight amusement.

'Young girls should not be falling into wells. They are too
dark and too deep. And the flower fields are a long way off
too. Start with the small things first, Teresa. Remember, you
still have time. Now off you go to sleep.'

Teresa said nothing. Her tongue had been tied into one
of those bouts of numbed silences.

Before getting into bed Teresa untied her hair. She looked at
what was in her hands. It was a white-laced handkerchief.
She brought it up to her nose to smell the flowers out in the
fields, and her mind floated into greenery and a

kaleidoscope of scented colours. She placed the handkerchief in her beside drawer for the morning. Teresa slipped beneath the bed sheets and with a slowed beating of her heart managed to find once more the gentle hand of sleep.

CHAPTER EIGHT

~ Flowers are the spontaneous expression of the sacred ~

Tibia was the first to notice the white-laced handkerchief. She had seen the next day that there was a different look to Teresa. With the hair pulled back from her face it made the young Teresa look older. Or maybe it was that the eyes were now more dominant, and you met with them first before moving across to her other features. And there was something, a little something else too that Tibia couldn't find words for. Yet when she watched her young friend move, and posture her body, she saw that it was there. And maybe Teresa noticed it too, but she never said anything.

True to her word, La Madre created a new game for the young girls – a game of flower cards. Many different varieties of flowers had been drawn onto cards, with their names and attributes written underneath. Two copies of each flower card were made, and the young girls would sit in a circle each placing a card in the middle. As each girl in turn around the circle would take a card from the middle, or from the pack, and place another card in the middle, the object was to collect pairs of the same flower – or a family of flowers in the same colour. In this way the young girls familiarised themselves with all the varieties of the flowers, from the fields and elsewhere. And the 'joker' card was the flower that did not exist in nature – but first they had to find it. It was Abigail, a seven year old girl, who spotted it first…

'It's the blue rose!' she had cried out triumphantly, and snatched the card to her chest. Her long, straight blonde hair swayed like wheat stalks as she ran off with the card to have her finding confirmed.

And it was true – a true blue pigment could not be produced by the rose in nature. And so the blue rose card could be chosen by the player to be any other flower they wished it to be. And yet the most important flower card in the pack was the *crocus sativus* – the saffron flower. There were three of these cards in the pack, and whoever could collect all three original cards would win the game outright. And no blue rose cards were allowed to substitute.

The young girls would play the flower card game each day after their morning studies, as their minds opened up to the eager energies between them. Teresa, Tibia, Alicia, and Abigail became fast friends. Yet Tibia and Teresa were closer to each other, being of the same age.

Every Tuesday and Thursday afternoons La Madre continued to come to the playground to talk to the young girls after gymnastics class. It was a harmony of activities that touched upon their youthful bodies and minds to sculpture new pathways. Restless energy and curiosity where channelled into forms more acceptable to digest. The world was unfolding in more subtle ways; in ways that young minds could grasp and process without the brashness or harshness that usually comes through the institutions that govern the youthful years of a human life.

When the next Thursday evening came around, as was the way now with the young girls, they waited expectantly for the figure of La Madre to emerge from the wooden door that led from the building to the playground. For some it was her smile they wished to see, as La Madre moved her glance slowly across the group. Each child felt as if the look was for them alone, a private moment of connection. Each child's keen eyes would be eagerly reaching out for the recognition; for the visual thread of acknowledgement and the smile. But not Teresa, who often turned her head slightly to the side to avoid the necessity of what she felt was a crude form of contact. For Teresa, La Madre was always present, like a speck of the invisible within the light. The world of the tangible is necessary for those who take their rewards from the tangible.

La Madre carefully seated herself and smoothed out the lines upon her white dress as would a calm breeze across the sea. The topic for this day was individual effort. La Madre's words were caught in the air and delivered to each child as a private gift. Teresa listened as the words landed upon the outer ridge of her ears and stepped within.

'The effort which you make individually will not remain only upon an individual level – it will spread, spread out!' and La Madre opened her arms wide as if catching the sunlight. 'It will spread and help all those around you. Never underestimate the potential within each individual – within each of you. Self-discipline is indispensable to you as an individual – it allows you to be free from the discipline imposed upon you from others in life. This freedom we can then share with those around us, who need it also. And supreme self-discipline is the same as sincere surrender. Just like the flowers surrender to Nature – they bend to the wind and give to the insects.'

La Madre reached into her folded blouse and brought out the prettiest of flowers. Teresa's eyes brightened as she gazed upon the pretty purple flower with bits of yellow and red dangling inside. She recognized it immediately from their flower card games. It was the crocus sativus – the saffron flower. La Madre smiled as she felt the ripple of recognition pass through the group of young attentive faces.

'Each thing has its own nature. Each thing can be discovered for what it truly is – just like the flower. Flowers are the spontaneous expression of the sacred. Flowers, such as the saffron here, respond to our creative imagination – they soak in our fantastical thoughts. And yet the saffron flower teaches us its charm, its wordless prayer – there is a special speech in silence.'

A silence slipped across the mouth of each girl bringing a shared wordless communion to the gathering. And yet inside each child another bud had begun to unfold, awaken, and to grow.

CHAPTER NINE

~ We carry the deep unconsciousness within us,
within our bodies, our memories, just as the earth
carries it in her minerals and her stones ~

The earth is cool and welcoming. It flows across Teresa's body as would a new garment discovering its owner for the first time. Yet it is heavier than cloth, denser than cotton, and its filaments are alive. Teresa twitches her fingers ever so slightly and the earth comes to fill the gap between them. There is no retreat from the soil. It presses against her youthful chest, enough to make its presence felt, not enough to cause discomfort. She knows she must consider the soil, the earth, as her friend…her guardian. She cannot fight against it. A few final drops of soil are sprinkled across her face – and then she is left completely alone in the darkness.

The earth breathes in rhythm to her own breathing,

signalling its companionship. There is nothing that separates them. The skin of her body is bathed in the cool earth. Eyes closed…feeling…sensing…remembering…

…there was that night when Teresa couldn't sleep, and so she had crept quietly out of the dormitory and outside into the starry summer night. Lying down upon the grass she had gazed up at the fine smoky trails of nebulae draped across the curved sky. She remembered thinking it was like a curtain across her world, and everything could vanish if it moved just an almost unperceivable step to the side. The world, she thought, was contained in that slice – a slice so thin it contained only her world. She had gazed up into the star-pinned sky for a long time, willing with her mind for it to shift into another sky, another world, into something other…

…but she had not been strong enough. And so Teresa remained fixed, stuck, in that slice of jellied life…like an insect preserved in precious stone…

The soft soil was beginning to sense her presence now and to send some patches of warmth through to her body. They were in correspondence and in the closeness of touch, of naked earth against skin, which stimulated the flow of memories. Time was moving in reverse, coursing through the capillaries of her stored sensations and secrets, delving into the tiniest of cavities within her where Teresa thought no one could go, not even herself.

And yet there was less and less of *herself*…there was something that was all – the blood, the tissue, the cells, the bone, the muscle…all the tiny electrical sparks that flickered simultaneously through the body as beacon lights, as niche of lights…

…there was just so much to recollect, to accept, and to give up…

Teresa was sitting on a bench in the corridor outside of late morning class. She had been agitated and this had led to restlessness. She could neither study nor cease from disturbing the friends around her. Teresa had been sent outside so that the only person she could now disturb was herself. The corridor was painted brick and had a high ceiling. Slight semi-circular arches were interspersed across the roof of the corridor like vertebra ripples down a spine. Some of the high plaster work was peeling off, giving the impression of dry skin flaking away from the body. The building was old, and it seemed to Teresa that it was observing her. She closed her eyes and inhaled deeply, allowing time to creep in with the shaded fragments of air. If

Teresa had imagined herself to be somewhere when she was a little older, it would not have been here. She shuffled her feet upon the stone floor at the same time as she tapped her fingers upon the bench. An older girl passed her by and said nothing.

'Fine,' thought Teresa, 'you don't understand my world anyway.'

A couple of ants were struggling with something between them. In their fierce battle Teresa watched a world before her unfold in miniature. And yet she knew that for the two ants this was a struggle of life-sized proportions.

'You don't exist for them.' A voice came unexpectedly.

Teresa looked up into the face of La Madre, and for a split second she thought she was looking at herself.

'Yes.' Teresa's own voice came out as a soft whisper, almost a hiss.

'You are too far away from them to be noticed. You do not understand their world and nor they yours. And yet, as you can see, both worlds are so close to one another. Only a hand-length separates you from them. And yet, as a matter of perception, you are invisible to them.'

Teresa looked once more at the struggling ants and smiled at the thought.

'Yes, I thought you might like that – to be invisible.' La Madre motioned for Teresa to follow her as she moved away down the corridor. Together they walked out into a small courtyard where a stone fountain was bubbling and splashing. They sat on a shaded seat where Teresa's legs daggled.

Teresa remembered watching her dangling feet as La Madre spoke to her about patience. She was thinking that if she could remember the image of her swinging feet, she would always remember what La Madre was saying. In her mind she had her own game where she would match image with words. And it worked.

Teresa let the patience seep into her body as she pictured in her mind the image of her young feet dangling. Her body then eased a little and her mind sat back slightly, pulling away from the restless thoughts that had been crawling over it like worms. The earth around her was now warming up and becoming like a blanket or, as Teresa thought, like an overcoat at night. Her breathing eased, and seemed to cradle her mind as if wishing for more memories to be unearthed.

…by the time Teresa was eleven she knew the large orphanage stone building almost inside out. Except, that is, for the dormitories where the older girls slept and the rooms where they cultivated the saffron flowers. She would watch as the other girls carried the flowers back indoors in their woven baskets. Every day was a new picking during the harvest period, and the scent would carry in the air as perfumed dust.

Tibia noticed the pensive face that her best friend wore. And with Teresa's ever-growing long brown hair tied back with her favourite handkerchief, her expression sometimes got interpreted as a frown.

'Frowny face today, is it?'
Teresa turned to her friend and stuck out her tongue.
'You're even uglier when you do that!' Tibia laughed.
'Don't care.' Teresa too smiled a little and it took all her willpower not to laugh.
'A penny for your thoughts?'
'You don't have a penny.'
Tibia shrugged. 'I doubt if you have any thoughts worth buying anyway.'
'Yeah, well, I'm not selling.' Teresa paused. 'But I will share for free!'
The two girls walked out of one of the side gates and down the path away from the main building. Now that the girls were eleven they were allowed to explore more of the grounds. The girls didn't know how much of the land

belonged to the orphanage, yet they knew that they could walk as far as their eyes could see and still not leave the grounds. Teresa and Tibia took a path that meandered along a hedgerow toward a sheltered copse. It was a place they often liked to go and talk together. They had made some seats out of discarded wooden logs placed end to end. As they walked they sensed the air was heavy and damp. By the time they reached the copse they were sweating. They knew a storm was coming – a rush of air to invade the atmosphere and freshen up the dense skies.

Soon enough, heavy clouds closed in over them and a rumbling sound rolled in over the fields. The two girls sat down on their log seats and waited for the drops of rain to begin falling. Tibia shuffled her feet restlessly and ran her fingers through her short auburn hair. She had always preferred to have her hair cropped short, in contrast to Teresa's long, straight hair. The two of them were almost chalk and cheese – or blueberry and raspberry, as they liked to say.

'What do you think La Madre means when she says we all have the sacred inside of us?'

Teresa snapped a twig between her fingers. The sky had cracked open and rain was now beginning to fall in large blots. 'She says that we are all expressions of the sacred. And that we have a responsibility to express it.'

Tibia pulled a face. 'Fine. But how? She didn't give us any

instruction book!'

The two girls laughed. Tibia reached over and took Teresa's long pony-tail in her hands. She stroked the long flock of hair, darker than her own.

'You have hair like a horse!'

'Better than having hair like a boy's!'

As they giggled Tibia looked again at the white laced handkerchief that tied back Teresa's hair.

'You never did tell me where you got that handkerchief from…'

Teresa paused. 'It's an expression of the sacred…like this is!' Teresa jumped up from the log and ran out into the embrace of the rainstorm. She held her hands up high and began twirling. A twirling girl in the rain.

Tibia ran out to join her. Two twirling girls in the rain. They closed their eyes and let the rain pour over them; over their faces and down the column of their backs. The clothes stuck to their bodies in contrast to t heir arms that stretched upwards…

…Teresa could feel the wetness on her face, and the feeling of freedom, of joy, and of the sacred…she could remember…

…could still remember it now as the soil, not the rain, covered her face and her body. She remembered it all – the sensations, the feelings, the contact with the sacred space. And now these memories also soaked out of her and into the depths of the earth. Teresa was sharing herself with the body of the planet. She remembered also the words of La Madre … *All takes time, that's the natural way of things…everything takes time to create, time to happen.*

Time, and more time…earth time…to go inward…further inward…

La Madre's words are now with Teresa intimately, and her words also linger in the earth as if the dirt and microbes of the soil were the carriers of letters; a sodden language. *The practice of going inward is an aspect of the feminine…nurture it as the soil nurtures her living beings…going outward is a sign of the world, going inward is a mark of the soul…*

When Teresa was twelve she was caught stealing a bottle of fruit juice from supplies by Madam Celia. The older lady, with her distinguished red hair, had entered the supply room at the exact moment Teresa's hand had opened the bottle and lifted it to her lips.

If you were thirsty, why didn't you just ask?

It was a logical question that had been repeatedly asked. Yet Teresa didn't have a logical answer. She hadn't wanted to ask. Nor had she been particularly thirsty. She had only wanted to know if she could do it. Was it possible? It had been possible – yet there had also been consequences.

La Madre had looked at Teresa with a casual detachment, as if one thing was neither here nor was it there.

'There is an old saying which might be applicable in this situation – *Take what you want says god – but pay for it!*'

Teresa listened but did not react. Her back was bent down and her hands were in the soil. Planting a garden of seeds for one gulp of juice, muttered Teresa inwardly to herself.

'Things may not appear fair or just on the outside,' continued La Madre as she watched from a nearby bench, 'but everything finds its balance. Things which may appear in contradiction are often working together – just like the sun and the rain, and the light and the dark. Remember this, little Teresa - everything comes from the darkness. Everything is born of the darkness – that is why darkness is recognized as a "she." It is within the darkness where the hidden ways of creation can be found. Let your hands be a part of that!'

Teresa was not impressed – but she *did* listen. She always listened when La Madre spoke; and somehow the both of them knew that.

Later that day, after she had finished seeding and had washed up, Teresa quietly slipped down to the little stream that ran through the rear of the orphanage. Sitting down by herself she closed her eyes and listened to the sounds. She recognized the sounds of yellows, the hues of blues, the tinkling of light as it reflected off the water, and the sounds of small eddies as they twirled, like two young wet girls. She longed in her heart to move forward.

The image of La Madre stepped into her mind's flow as if stepping into the stream's current. *Life is given for a purpose and our task is to find that purpose and carry out our agreed task.* 'Why so much burden I have to carry?' Teresa had asked this question one day to La Madre.

'Don't be selfish, or naïve,' the elder lady had replied. 'It is not for you alone. And it is only those who carry this task shall find the burden, as you call it, lighter. The weight of ignorance is so much heavier. Now don't be a selfish girl. You didn't come here to be selfish – none of us did.'

With this in mind Teresa picked up a pebble and threw it into the stream before her. That pebble, she told herself, was for the mistake of being naïve and selfish. Teresa picked up another pebble. 'And this one's for the fruit juice,' she said quietly as she threw it into the stream.

One after another Teresa picked up a pebble and threw

it into the stream for each past mistake that lay upon her mind. The sun had begun to dip by the time Teresa had reached a place of silence. She felt empty now, but good. Somehow, without knowing why, the stream had diverted its course and ran through her young body, washing away the silt that had collected within Teresa over the years. And it felt fresh. Despite the warmth of the day she felt the goose bumps upon her legs and her tiny body hairs tingled.

Yes, she remembered it all now…it all came flooding through her…

And the earth continued to caress her as if she too was a small seed – like one of those she had planted by her own hands. If Teresa could have listened to her own truth she would have known she had indeed planted her own seed. Yet as she lay there she listened to the words of La Madre…

…*We carry the deep unconsciousness within us, within our bodies, our memories, just as the earth carries it in her minerals and her stones. There is a deep unknowing that resides within us, slumbering and yet watchful – waiting for our moments of attentiveness so that it may awake a little more…*

Perhaps that was why La Madre had placed Teresa under the earth, covered by a blanket of soil.

૫ᵃ

If Teresa had imagined herself to be somewhere when she was a little older, it would not have been here. She had just celebrated her thirteenth birthday only a few days before.

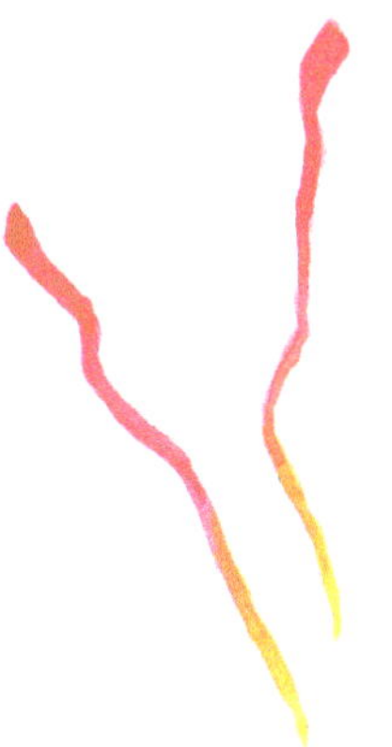

LA MADRE

*You are not here for your development – you are here
for your unfolding. You already contain the essence;
you cannot develop upon this, but you can allow it to
unfold and spread out in the most correct and
harmonious way.*

CHAPTER TEN

~ Transformation is contagious ~

Teresa had a different understanding of her memory. It was no longer a fixed picture that lay stuck in her mind as a dusty photo album. Now her memory, and all the identities associated with it, was a fluid stream that flowed through her mind and her body. Each incident was not a mark etched on stone but a finger placed into a current of water. The world outside of the Azafran Home for Girls had been a static place; small, grey, and occupied with its own trappings.

Teresa turned to her close friend Tibia and smiled. Tibia reached over and fingered the white laced handkerchief that tied back Teresa's long dark hair.

'What do you think La Madre's talk will be about today?'

'I think she'll ask for questions.'

Tibia giggled. 'You always like the questions. Why don't you ask her how old she is?'

Teresa shrugged. 'One day maybe I will.'

Teresa had finished her morning duties of helping the younger girls to clean their dormitory. Now that she was officially a teenager Teresa and her friends had been moved out of their old dormitory and replaced to another wing of the large building. Their new sleeping arrangements were smaller and Teresa now shared a room only with Tibia, Alicia, and Abigail. Over the years their friendship had grown closer whilst their personalities had grown apart. The remnants left over from the early years of their respective social backgrounds had begun to dissolve. The aspects they had been taught to conform to, those that had formed the outer cask of their personalities, were no longer fed or attended to, and so had withered as would a flower without water.

After finishing her duties with the younger children Teresa went outside to water the plants. The sun was a little cooler now as the season approached another zenith of its passing. There was something very essential to Teresa about getting her hands into the dirt. Merely watering the plants was not enough for her; she needed to feel the earthiness, the texture and soundless voice of the soil. She was one of the few girls who actually enjoyed weeding. Yet for Teresa these were enjoyable mornings. She took pleasure in the routine of the early rise with the sun, helping to prepare the breakfasts with the plump Madam Pym, helping to organize the younger girls, and then going out to tend the strips of gardens that ran around the large orphanage. She knew that routine was a form of order, and that daily order was a reflection of one's inner order. There was no such thing as boredom as far as Teresa was concerned. She recalled the incident where one morning, as Teresa was hard at work weeding an overgrown stretch of garden, La Madre had come by and stopped to watch. As Teresa's sweat-lined brow had looked up to acknowledge her La Madre smiled and said, 'It's good to see a person sweating.'

Teresa knew sweat well.

Gymnastics class was no longer the same. As younger girls they had recognized the familiarity of the moves they were asked to make. Now their bodies were being asked to contort in other ways and forms. They were forcing their bodies to stretch into postures and shapes none of the girls had known before. Their teacher, the same blond-haired Anna with her thin face, instructed the girls calmly and with patience. Anna spoke very little besides delivering her instructions. The girls knew that Anna would now be twenty-four years old; and they liked her.

After class the girls relaxed their bodies and waited for La Madre to arrive. Whilst her appearance was expected, her words never could be.

La Madre looked the same as ever. In Teresa's fluid memory there was no place for an image to become fixed and fade into old age. La Madre sat down in her favourite chair then placed her hands upon her lap and breathed calmly. When she looked up and observed the gathering of youthful faces before her a twinkle rippled across her eyes.

'What happens individually in your bodies will affect other bodies. What goes on inside you will spread out. Transformation is contagious. You will come to recognize that I speak quite a lot about contagion – but of the good kind!' La Madre allowed herself a quiet laugh, as if sharing an inner joke with the wind that browsed amongst the boughs. She leaned forward and winked at the girls. 'Why are we here?' Then she turned her head slightly to look directly at Abigail. 'Some of us have that exact question in our heads,' she continued, 'and so I say to you all that we are here to play the game, of course! Yet not any old game - a very specific game, with all the will power at our disposal. And it is important to know that we are supported in this game by a great amount of energy. Most people do not suspect the game exists – this is the sad part. If there's no game, there's no play. Yet for those who know, the question becomes *how* to play. It is not a 'normal' game, as we might suspect. It is far more precious, and exhilarating. So we must learn this game, and to act deliberately. This is the game that we call Life. Life is contagious and, as I have said, transformation is contagious. Yet for many people, they need a special ingredient in their lives.'

La Madre clasped her hands together and leaned back into her chair.
'Now then, who has a question for me?'

Silence. There were many questions hanging in the space of the gathering, within individual minds, yet they were being held back. Teresa brought her question to the forefront and let it sit there, singing out its sound – though she did not speak it. She knew that La Madre knew that she knew. Teresa concentrated on the shape of her question rather than upon its individual letters. She sensed that individual letters often got lost once out of the mouth, but the shape of a thought remained intact.

La Madre closed her eyes for a brief moment and nodded to herself.

'Yes, quite right - silence is often more useful than words. Why do I say that? Because the word is restricted – its meaning is received by each mind with limited flexibility. Each mind interprets words slightly differently according to the person's background and upbringing, which is their cultural framework. If such identity is not dissolved within a person, as dead leaves dissolve into the earth, then the inflexibility of words is caught within this framework. With silence this is different. Silence is received by each mind as a vibration and is interpreted by the inward being according to a person's state. Its meaning and message can be so much richer than that of words – and closer to the truth. Silence can give rise to an inner experience – a realization or epiphany. Silence has to be allowed to roam freely inside a person trustingly. One should not fight or struggle against silence. Perhaps this is why so many people find silence uncomfortable. Yet here we cultivate the art of listening to silence. It is like listening to the saffron flower as a gentle breeze moves along the edges of its petals. It is as if listening to something extremely subtle. To obtain an attentive silence is both a delicate and yet a most practical and important skill.'

After a short pause Tibia was the first to speak up. 'La Madre, what is an attentive silence like? How can it be achieved?' 'My dear, it is a subtle inner movement that allows you to be open and receptive so that you can receive all that is to be received. It is a space where all things of the outer world do not stir. It is a space within the self that is both deeply still and yet active at the same time. It is a space that knows no contradiction and where the flame of knowing burns as bright as running water. Each person must seek and find this space for themselves.'

La Madre made a soft yet deliberate tapping movement with her fingers upon her lap. She then briefly glanced over at Teresa who felt something like an invisible dart enter into her eye.
'Perhaps your burning question,' continued La Madre, 'is when shall you begin to pick the saffron flowers, which brings us nicely back to the game of contagious life, and its *special ingredient*. This is the nature of the spice. But before we are ready for such things, we must learn the art of a lesser game - the game of the crystal bowl.'

The four girlfriends sat quietly in their room as they prepared to get ready for the closing of the day. They felt sleepy, as they did each evening before crawling into their beds and closing their eyes. Each day was a blend of work duties, physical exercise, and educational lessons. And yet the environment also provided something more, something *extra* that went beyond what could be seen, heard, touched, or felt. Each girl knew this, even if they didn't know they knew it; or if they didn't have the words for it. It is not always necessary to articulate something – only to recognize it.

Alicia was combing Abigail's long blonde hair. Both girls had blonde hair, yet Alicia's was cropped at the shoulders. Teresa was sitting on her bed watching this practice, as she had watched so many times before. Often Tibia would comb her own long dark hair after she had taken out the white laced handkerchief. Teresa liked to watch hands at play; delicate fingers moving and weaving, touching and sensing. Abigail looked over and smiled at Teresa.

'Deep in thought again?'

'Watching the world go by,' answered Teresa.

'I don't believe that! Or at least not the normal world.' Both Abigail and Alicia laughed in a gentle way. 'Your world is somewhere else. It always has been for as long as I've known you.'

'Mmm. My world had to be somewhere else. I never had a choice.'

'Everyone has a choice,' interrupted Alicia.

'No. Sometimes real choices are given upon you and you can't decide if you want it or not. I think real freedom comes from having no choice.'

'I don't understand…'

Teresa smiled over at her friend Alicia. She liked her, as she liked all her friends. And one day she knew that she would have no choice but to distance herself from them. 'Some things have to be done because they're correct. There's no choice in the matter, it's just how it is.'

Suddenly Tibia walked into the room with her toothbrush still in her mouth. She mumbled something that made no sense. All the other three girls looked at her oddly. Tibia pulled the toothbrush out of her mouth and grinned.

'I was saying, are you all ready for our meeting with La Madre tomorrow?'

CHAPTER ELEVEN

*~ We are not interested in perfection - We work with
the frailties ~*

The four girls were seated outside of La Madre's room, each in her own silence. All the girls of their age had been called to make the visit, each dormitory room at a time. Madam Aisha, the personal secretary to La Madre, opened the door and motioned for the girls to enter. It was an autumnal morning, and a haze of light lay across the stone floor. Teresa inhaled deeply as she entered, remembering herself and where she was. The memory of her first visit to this room as a young five year old girl was a memory that now dwelled within the earthly soil and dirt. The moment now was as fresh and alive as Nature's kiss upon each blade of grass as it sang its song sweetly.

The four girls sat on chairs arranged around a small wooden table. They all faced La Madre who sat opposite them in her large upholstered chair. Placed on the small wooden table was what looked like a crystal bowl, and next to it lay its lid. La Madre opened her hands in a gesture of welcome and gave a warm smile.

'My dear young girls, my soon-to-be saffron collectors; you are each of you a drop of spice.'

Tibia, Alicia, and Abigail all responded with a collective giggle, as if an angel feather had reached inside to tickle them. Teresa though remained silent and looked firmly at the crystal object.

'At next season's harvest you shall all have the opportunity, I hope, to participate in the gathering of the spice. It is a very delicate process, and steady hands are required.' La Madre looked slowly at each of the four girls. 'And steady hearts too, for all hands are but extensions of our hearts. And our hearts are but extensions of the spice, which flows through everything. A saffron collector must be both delicate and heartfelt in their touch, as if reaching out for the very essence of an unborn soul. So…let's start here shall we?'

La Madre reached out her slender hand and gracefully picked up the crystal lid and with a flowing movement placed it upon the top of the bowl. With a wave of her hand she picked it up and placed it on the table again. 'There we are, simple as that. Who would like to have a go?'

After a slight pause Abigail reached over to the table and picked up the crystal lid. With a slow movement she placed it on top of the bowl. As soon as she had done so a soft yet clear ringing vibration reverberated in the air.

La Madre smiled. 'The crystal bowl sings. She sings in response to your own vibration. Each of us is ringing out in each moment, even if we do not hear our own song.' La Madre placed the crystal lid back on the table and nodded to Alicia who was seated next to Abigail.
Alicia lifted the lid ever so gently and placed it on the bowl. Again, the crystalline vibration rang out.
Alicia pouted. 'But I put it on ever so carefully.'
'I know, my dear. Yet the ringing you have is inside of you. When you reach out for the lid you must do so from your own inner space of silence. Quieten yourself first before making contact with the bowl.'

All four girls sat in silence. Tibia was next. After a minute or so Tibia reached forward and made the same gesture. And yet again the crystal bowl rang out. Tibia pulled a face and sat back. La Madre silently returned the crystal lid to the table. Then it was time for Teresa's turn. With utmost concentration Teresa carefully reached for the lid and with as much grace as was possible for her slight hands she lightly placed it upon the crystal bowl.

Everyone listened.

Nothing…then a tiny ringing reached their ears…the vibration of gentle glass shards.

La Madre nodded and gave a slight motherly smile. 'No one achieves silence the first time. Not to worry. You have all made an excellent beginning. We are not interested in perfection; we work with the frailties. No one begins from completion – it is a destination and not a starting point. Only that some of us have a better start in this.' A slither of sunlight appeared to bounce off La Madre's eyes and made them sparkle. Or perhaps it was a reflection from the crystal bowl, a shimmering of a glass shard that caught a stray ray of light and flicked it on.

A magical quality infused the room as would the scent of a wind-blown flower, or a passing stranger's perfume. Teresa half-closed her eyes so that she could sense the periphery, that ephemeral border that blurs between one reality and another. And as Teresa relaxed her focus and softened her mind a vibratory dance of colour swept across her vision. La Madre was no longer the older lady seated in the chair across from her, but a haze of what Teresa could only describe as a pulsating energy, radiating in shades of blue. Teresa began to feel dizzy as she tried to see through unfocused eyes. So she closed them, and went inside. She took a step into her inner homeland, to where she knew dwelt a place of silence. She could hear with an inner sense the faint chimes of crystal as if it were a voice whispering in song. Then she heard voices again.

When Teresa opened her eyes she saw that La Madre was listening to a question from one of the other girls. Yet Teresa was not able to focus fully on the words, or to make the sounds into intelligible carriers of meaning. La Madre shifted a quick glance over to Teresa, with a sudden movement of the head, and Teresa felt a spike of energy rush into her that made her body sit upright.

La Madre coughed as if to speak. 'The saffron collector must not only work with their hands but also with their presence…with their personal essence. Their hands have to be firm, steady, and yet gentle. And their presence should be silent, as if absorbed in a pool of cool energy. If we make a sound, we impress that sound into the quality of the saffron, and thus we may pollute it a little. Our role, as saffron collectors, is to channel something *other than us* into the process of gaining the spice. The spice is then a carrier for a special ingredient that can be mixed with the delicious dishes of the world. Yet we must work with the saffron as if transparent, empty…like a crystal vessel. And we should be careful that we do not impress *our* sounds into the essence of the spice.'

La Madre lifted up the lid from the crystal bowl and placed it on the table, and without waiting she swiftly placed it back onto the bowl. She waited, fingers in silence. A bird song erupted outside and spilled into the room. Nothing more. La Madre continued the same process several times, each time quicker than the previous. Her hands moved like graceful threads weaving an invisible tapestry into the air around her. All the time there was an incredible stillness of soundlessness.

'You shall arrive at this,' said La Madre finally, as she placed her hands gently upon her lap. 'Yet first there are other things before you. The next planting will be in the springtime.' La Madre turned her head away to the side. Teresa noticed how delicate her ears were, as if sculptured intricacies added later to the head.

CHAPTER TWELVE

*~ As soon as a person stops moving forward, they
begin to take a step back ~*

Madam Celia kept her hair coloured red despite her age. There were times when the grey roots would show through and start to grow, as if displaying their own defiance against the colouring. Yet Madam Celia always kept her hair in good order, just like her supply room. Teresa had formed a good relationship with Madam Celia, which she put down to the incident of stealing the fruit juice when she was younger. Sometimes, it seemed, events occurred for reasons other than they appear at the time. Or, as Madam Celia liked to say, 'everything is a catalyst for something else – whatever that may be!'

One of Teresa's responsibilities was to work in the supply store, managing orders, stock, and basically controlling what came in and what went out. Teresa was good at this because she had a strong memory of things, and where they should be, and how much of any one thing there was, or needed to be. Madam Celia was a practical lady, tall and slim, and with a thinish face that could be seen as stern if one was to stare for too long. Yet Teresa was not a person for staring, and she had soon come to realize that Madam Celia had a very dry sense of humour.

Teresa was looking through one of the storerooms, checking off items on her pad when she heard some muttering from behind. She turned to see Madam Celia shaking her head and tutting as if to herself.

'You girls use more toilet paper than bread. How can that be?

'We have higher priorities than hunger…' Teresa smiled back.

'Bodily needs are what the body needs, I suppose.' Madam Celia flicked through one of her record books as if working. But Teresa knew better than that, so she kept her ears open.

'And what life needs right now is more of the feminine…if it's ever going to be prepared for the real change to come.' Madam Celia clucked her tongue and continued to turn the pages without looking up. 'I suppose the danger,' she continued, 'is when the exterior world only reflects back upon itself, expanding upon the bad things, and not revealing what lies beyond. And the exterior is just so masculine and heavy…need a bit of the feminine…' Madam Celia clucked again. 'We've got to bring back things from the unseen to the seen, from non-activity to activity.' Finally Madam Celia raised her head and looked ahead of her, but not directly at Teresa. Instead it was as if she were talking to herself, yet knowing Teresa was in the room. 'By making things active you make them alive in the world. And something special enters through the heart when the feminine is active. First it may destroy before it can rebuild. Then the softest can overcome the hardest; the most subtle can transform the coarsest. The light within one awakens the light within another – this is the transmission. Teresa!'

Teresa's attention bolted upright as Madam Celia turned to look directly at her.
'Yes?'
'Order some more toilet paper. We can't have ladies being left in the lurch! And some more bread too, if you wish…' The older lady turned and walked out of the room as if there was nothing more to be said.

Yet Teresa had had ears to hear. For the rest of the morning she fulfilled her stock duties.

It was important to get stocked up for the coming months. Autumn was fading and a winter chill was edging ever closer. Teresa remembered the winters well. She knew about snow from her earliest years, yet snow did not fall at the Azafran Home for Girls. The soil hardened with frost, and then softened with rain; and winds blew around the high walls and corners of the old building. And yet snow did not fall. The discomfort came from the dampness. It was like a wet hand coming through the skin and closing around the bones. It was even more imperative in winter that one did the gymnastics, if only to keep the body warm and everything inside circulating.

Teresa made the entries into the order book. Besides the toilet paper and the bread, Teresa made a note for as many lemons as possible to be collected from the trees. Lemons in winter were important.

There were places in the large orphanage building where Teresa liked to walk alone. It was always possible to find time alone despite having full days of activities and duties. There was work duties in the mornings, such as in the breakfast kitchens; then classes up until midday where some of the older children, now Teresa's age, would help again in the kitchens to prepare the meals. In the afternoons there were various assignments, or exercises; or the girls were left to do their own things which, for Teresa, meant going for long walks outside in the fields. The only places she could not yet visit were the saffron fields. It was not yet her time for that. She also liked the sparse rooms at the far top of the orphanage where old objects were kept stored.

In one of the large rooms was her favourite tapestry. It hung from the wall in glorious faded colours. For Teresa it was like a map, a coded terrain. A map of places her mind had not yet travelled to. She liked to stand in front of the tapestry and gaze at it until her eyes softened and the smell of aged material crept into her nostrils. Teresa decided to once again climb the many stairs that took her to the tapestry room. Upon entering she walked over to the tapestry and ran her fingers over the stitched patterning, feeling, sensing, as if discerning a different alphabet, a different form of language. As she did so a cluster of images emerged in her mind, rearranging themselves into a chain…an unfolding story…

Teresa thought she heard a faint voice call out. She came back to her regular senses and looked around the room. And yet she was alone. Following her instinct she walked towards the window and looked down upon the grass lawn. She almost froze. Below on the grass stood La Madre, moving slowly in a deliberate yet strange manner. She was not walking normally but stepping to the side, taking a few steps then turning at right angles to make another few steps. It showed a deliberate if somewhat awkward pattern. Teresa watched as it seemed that La Madre was repeating the same pattern. After several repeated moves La Madre suddenly stopped. She slowly turned around and looked up directly into Teresa's face. Yet Teresa was not looking at La Madre. She abruptly jerked back in shock, her breathing caught in her throat as a constricted gasp. She stepped away from the window. No, it must have been a trick of the eyes.

Teresa turned and left the room. Her mind was now shaking as if her thoughts were hurriedly re-arranging themselves into some new cohesion. Even her thoughts too, they told her, had been shocked. How could it be? Surely she could not have seen her own face staring back at her from La Madre? Surely…

The thirteen-year-old girl that was known as Teresa walked hurriedly back down the corridors of the large building of the Azafran Home for Girls. She knew the corridors well having walked them for many years. And so it was with some disbelief that Teresa suddenly realized that she was where she should not be. Yet where had she made the wrong turns? Before her mind could make the necessary re-adjustments Teresa realized she was on the corridor that led past La Madre's private quarters. It was a place she should not be – and yet she was.

She walked past the door to La Madre's room and saw that it was open. She stopped. And then it happened. Something within her compelled her to return to the open door. The same compelling force urged her to walk through the door and into La Madre's private quarters.

She stepped towards the door. Then a sudden force of hesitancy welled up within her that tugged at her bodily impulse and gave her doubt. Teresa automatically took a step back. Then she heard the voice of La Madre.
'As soon as a person stops moving forward, they begin to take a step back.'

Teresa took a step forward. And then another.

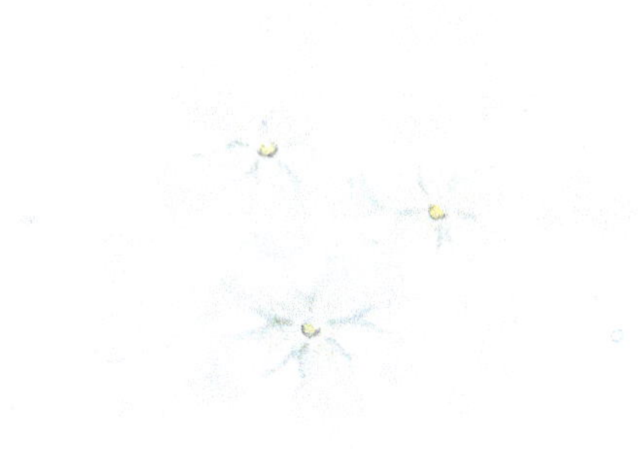

CHAPTER THIRTEEN

~ Treat your words as if they were your children ~

A smoky scent drifted across the room; a perfumed haze. Teresa recognized that an incense stick was burning somewhere, effusing its fragrance among the molecules of the air. Before she had even turned around she knew La Madre was behind her, sitting at a table to one side of the open door.

'You may close it now. Closed doors attract no mosquitoes.'

Teresa turned and closed the door, moving as naturally as she could. She was trying to remain calm despite a deep pounding within her. She finally looked at La Madre, only to be met by downward eyes as the older lady was sipping a cup of tea. On the table beside the teapot was placed a second teacup, empty and waiting for another hand, another mouth. La Madre lifted her eyes and motioned for Teresa to sit down at the table. As she sat she sensed another perfume, this one light and subtle.

'Would you care for a cup of tea, Teresa? I think you would like this particular flavour.'

Teresa hesitated and before she could answer La Madre smiled sweetly. 'It isn't saffron tea. We don't do saffron in everything - otherwise you'd all be eating saffron bread and saffron cookies!' This time the older lady gave out a little laugh and her delicate face radiated a warmth that helped Teresa to relax. 'Pour yourself a cup of jasmine tea.'

Teresa sat back in her chair and sipped the tea, trying not to be seen observing how slight and youthful seemed La Madre's fingers. For a while both ladies – young and old – sat in silence as if in ceremony. Teresa knew that unlike herself, La Madre did not need to observe her physically from without. No doubt, she thought, she was already an open book, an easy read.

Finally, La Madre made a gentle sigh; a tone of satisfaction, as if she was pleased with the tea. Then she spoke softly. 'You came here because of yourself, not because of anyone else. Do not fool yourself over this, Teresa. You found my door open because there was an assent from both sides. My door does not open for those whom are not ready to enter. *You must do that work first.'*

Teresa tilted her head slightly, yet did not feel as if she had a response.

'One must listen to the feeling of assent we have within each of us. It is a subtle feeling inside the chest, near the solar plexus. It also shows us when something is against the essential self. We can feel its assent; likewise, we can feel its silent voice when it speaks out against our actions and thoughts. It is a lighthouse that shines no light, and yet guides us. It guides us against our doubts that often jump up into us at the last minute, trying to make a big splash and distract us. Just like you felt in that moment of hesitation before entering through the door.'

Teresa blushed slightly, yet maintained her focus upon La Madre's expression.

'The shadows of doubt are not necessarily bad for us. They can help us define the light of the truth. They show to us the obstacles that are placed in our path. They provide contrasts, and it is from these that we can see the definitions more clearly of where the light is, where it is not; and importantly, those places which lack the *essential* - that lack the spice.'

A thought suddenly erupted into Teresa's mind. 'I really wish to move forward,' she said in a slight voice. Then for a second time, in a stronger voice, 'I need to move forward. I have to do this.'

'Is that a promise?'

Teresa nodded.

'We each must work with our promises – when we give a promise it must be accomplished. We may postpone it, yet to fail to deliver upon it will only reflect back badly upon the person. If you use words, you should stand by them – they are your children, your responsibility. Treat your words as if they were your children.'

This last phase made Teresa smile. She liked it. She always liked the way La Madre spoke. It was simple, and yet it made so much sense to her.

'I like listening to you. There's this goodness when you speak.' Teresa suddenly felt a little embarrassed. The words had just come from her mouth; they had spilled out like naughty children. Yet she was glad she had said them. There had been so few times when Teresa was able to express herself intimately with La Madre.

La Madre leaned forward and reached out for Teresa's hands. She took the small hands in her own and covered them in a ball of wrapped fingers. Teresa felt comfort and security, as if protected from everything else when in La Madre's hands.

'Goodness lies deep within all things and can be found, if

sought.'

'But I don't always see it in others.' Teresa let a small sigh escape her.

'Do not concern yourself with the faults of others; observe them, and then allow this reflection to come back upon yourself. Recognition of our own self comes from the recognition of others. Trust in yourself, and what you represent.'

'What *I* represent?'

La Madre smiled and gazed deeply upon the young girl's face. 'What *we* represent. There is something subtle that exists within the feminine, and it is very strong at the same time. Such a thing as feminine power cannot be seen clearly - it is not something that is seen but rather something that is veiled. And that which is concealed can achieve a lot more than that which is visible. It is better for us this way. We can work more effectively when it is least suspected. This is the way of the saffron.'

Teresa smiled inwardly, recognizing something that she had always known. A presence that had been with her from deepest time; from deepest roots, and which always called upon her gently, as if a breeze, a whisper, an untouching touch.

Teresa never forgot that time with La Madre; a moment of mutual assent over the jasmine tea…an instance of splendid isolation where the world was pushed away from intervening.

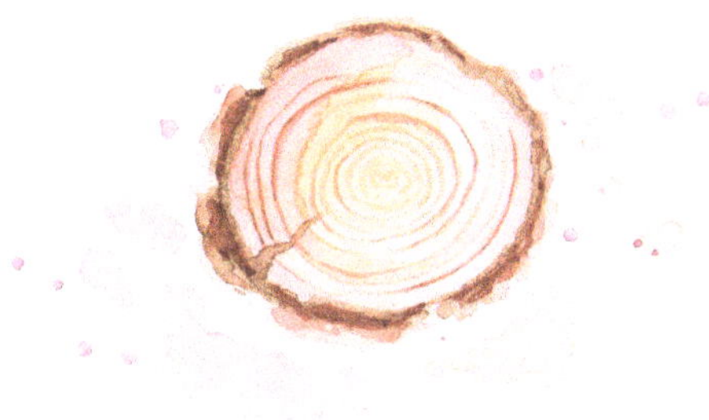

CHAPTER FOURTEEN

~ We are all fools – yet some of us are conscious fools ~

The winter rains came as expected. And Teresa had turned fourteen. The dry soil soaked up the drops of water like a thirsty desert dweller. Teresa could feel within her own bones how the soil felt as it drank deeply from the rains. Her own body had shared this experience with the soil the previous year. Both bodies had mixed and partaken of each other as twin sisters, with open mouths, open souls. The rains were falling again, touching the flesh of the Mother Earth, and everything was felt to be in its place.

Winter came as it did across all the lands. Yet the Azafran Home for Girls was situated within the more temperate Mediterranean climate, and the transitions from summer to winter, and back again, were relatively moderate. No snow, no extremes; just the subtler changes within Nature.

Some of the girls shivered as the large stone rooms radiated the cold that came to wrap itself around the large outside walls. Some of the other girls muttered that the orphanage was not built for winter, only for summer and sun. Teresa would shake her head and remain silent. It wasn't the seasonal comments she disagreed with – it was the reference to the place as an orphanage. An orphanage was a place for orphans. And orphans were those who were without parents. And yet here they were, with family, and with a new mother – La Madre. The Azafran Home for Girls was, for Teresa, just that…a home. And they were not orphans – they were collectors. And right now Teresa and her friends, the newest group of teenagers, were waiting for their first harvest of spice.

The large wood furnace in the basement, or *sótano*, as the Madams preferred to call it, raged with heated fury that warmed the rooms and corridors of the stone-bodied house. Stove pipes ran through the rooms to share and spread the warmth, and experienced hands fed the fire with chopped wood daily. Energy from the hand of Nature mingled with the seasonal change to create a different ambiance around the large building. Teresa noticed it, and knew it was not an inconvenience, merely a *difference*. And within this difference the talks with La Madre took on an altered character too.

The gymnastics classes were still outside, weather permitting, yet the talks afterwards were in the Reception Room, with La Madre seated upon her upholstered chair beside a small wood-stacked stove. The energy of the room embraced the youngsters with a touch of interior warmth different from that of the rays of the sun.

La Madre, seated by the stove, sipped from a teacup already prepared for her. Teresa didn't need to wait for the perfumed smell to reach her senses; she already knew what tea it was. Sometimes the taste still lingered upon the memory corpuscles of her tongue.

'There is a very particular energy in Nature,' began La Madre once she had lowered the teacup. 'There is a web of life, of energy and light, which surrounds the Earth and is of great power. This energy flows through and across the Earth - plants and Nature act as antennas to direct this energy. This web of life has always been present. Since the dawn of history it has been used for healing, for connecting, and for transmitting energy to specific locations. Time and energy have specific relationships, which are not always the same. Most people are familiar with what is called world time, or planetary time. Alongside this we work also with something we may refer to as *effective* time. By this, I mean a space in time which has been specifically influenced by the past time and which is having a marked effect on the future time. This relation between past, present and future can exist within a deliberate lock-on of energy. To put it as simply as is possible,' said La Madre with a slight smile, 'it enables a person with the right tools to influence a specific location at a specific time.'

Yes, the spice thought Teresa.

'Such tools, in our terms of reference, refer to the collection and dissemination of the saffron spice.' La Madre glanced over to Teresa. 'First of all,' continued La Madre, 'we need to place ourselves in the correct state for using such tools.' La Madre then threw a quick glance over to Alicia. 'How do you find our home?'

Alicia shrugged, unsure of the direction of the question. 'Well, I don't think it's a normal place.'

Most of the other girls laughed. Abigail poked Alicia in the ribs playfully. La Madre laughed too and nodded her head. 'Mais oui, bien sûr!'

Tibia raised her hand and La Madre motioned her to speak.

'Is this place somehow central to the flows in this web of energy?'

'Yes and no,' replied La Madre without hesitation. 'Let us start with something even closer to home – you! Never doubt that this energy, this web of life, surges through you - remember you are always deeply connected. However, it is crucial to make the energy collective. If we keep what we have, each for ourselves – if the energy stays individual – then it will not work for you. We must offer ourselves in service - offering ourselves is the only way of keeping the energy going. Then we become a channel for the *special ingredient* that is the spice. Yet we must give a part of ourselves. After all, the spice accepts you – you don't accept the spice.' La Madre raised her finger to indicate that she was going to say something that everyone should take note of. The hushed silence fell even deeper, and not even the crackles of flames from the stove could be heard. 'When you are collecting the saffron spice, it may feel like you own it. But once it accepts you, it *owns you!* And then you have no choice but to serve it. When you arrive at that moment you must be willing to make the choice. You will choose a direction and surrender to the process. And if the saffron flower accepts to give you her spice then you are going to start to feel connected to something that will forever guide your actions. The deeper you connect, the more knowing comes.'

Tibia raised her hand again. 'And what if the saffron flower doesn't accept me? I've never been good in the gardens…' This time everybody laughed, and poor Tibia blushed in embarrassment. She thought it had been a reasonable question, after all. She turned to her friends and made a girly face. 'Yeah, I guess I'm the fool this time.'
'We are all fools,' replied La Madre over the din of giggles, 'yet some of us are conscious fools.'

Then the sound of crackling wood flames returned, as if allowed back into the world…or rather, into the world of the Azafran Home for Girls.

CHAPTER FIFTEEN

*~ There is nothing nobler than the inward recognition
of two souls ~*

The morning rituals could sometimes be fun. All the dormitories on the floor shared a large communal bathroom. Girls would queue, giggling, with toothbrushes in their mouths and towels over their shoulders. There were sometimes the sleepy heads, the droopy eyelids, and the tired faces. And almost invariably there would be the whispers…the speculations…the fantasies. Yet it was an orderly energy – a harmonious energy. La Madre had said very early on that there were no fixed forms, no fundamentalism of behaviour: the only one abiding rule was harmony. Every step taken, she had once said, must be a step walked with harmony. Yet La Madre had said nothing about gossip and the odd teasing.

The inhabitants of each room had to organize and clean their own space. Each morning after the bathroom visit the girls would make their beds and tidy their room. Tibia was famous for being last, and late, from the bathroom. The other girls in the room – Abigail, Alicia, and Teresa – were now accustomed to Tibia's habits, although it didn't stop them from teasing her about it. With her short brown hair and her rounded face, Tibia could sweet smile anyone into forgiving her.

'Tibia-come-lately has just come into the room.' Abigail chuckled as Tibia stuck out her tongue.

'Better late than never.' Tibia whistled, or rather she tried to whistle as she wasn't very good at that.

'Unless it's your own funeral,' added Alicia.

'If it's my own funeral I'd rather be very late, very, very late – like kinda never!' All the girls laughed as they continued to tidy the room. 'Anyhow, I may be the last back from the bathroom, but Teresa's always the last one to speak. I guess everyone's got to be last in something. What about you, what are you last in?'

Abigail shrugged. 'Maybe I'm the last one to know what La Madre is talking about.'

'Well,' interrupted Alicia, 'I'm certainly the last to know

what the hell is going on around here!' Abigail and Alicia embraced each other as they both smiled and gave each other a sweet kiss on the cheek. Tibia walked over and put her arms around the two girls and joined in their embrace. Teresa remained sitting on her tidy, made bed. She recognized something special in her friends. They were family; a bond beyond blood, beyond the flesh body of life.

Teresa and Tibia were quietly looking together through a shelf of books in the building's library. Teresa already had several books in her hand which she gave to Tibia to hold. After finding a couple of more books Teresa indicated it was time to leave. They left the library and walked to the floor above where one of the large common rooms was situated. The large salon room was almost empty. They went over to a sofa and sat down, placing the books on a low table.

'You should read these, they'll be good for you.'

Tibia looked over at her friend Teresa. 'Why do we have to read so much?'

'Learning is a skill.'

Tibia pulled a face. 'But I've learned gymnastics and gardening, although I'm not very good at it!'

Teresa patted her friend's arm. 'Everything is a skill we will need. It all comes together – body *and* mind. There are certain ways of thinking that will help us. You know, like putting new wine into old bottles.'

'We're not old, Teresa, we're only fourteen.'

Teresa sighed and pinched her friend. 'You know it's a metaphor, you dumb donkey.'

Tibia reached over and hugged Teresa. 'And this dumb donkey loves you. And when you're all grown-up and Madre-like, I'll still love you even though you'll be giving me orders.'

Teresa pulled back slightly. 'Why do you say that?'

'Because you know it's so. Things just are. And you are who you are, or who you're going to be.'

'Maybe you don't need these books after all.'

'Nope, I got my instinct! But…' Tibia picked up one of the books and leaned back in the sofa and began reading.

CHAPTER SIXTEEN

~ Remembrance is one of our greatest steps ~

A new year had arrived in glorious fashion. The first day of the New Year was bright sunshine and a buffet was arranged for the outside patio. All the girls, young and older, were in high spirits. It was a good sign for the year ahead. Many of the older girls whispered that it was going to be a warm year, which meant that it would be a good saffron harvest. The rains so far had been moderate, and now the hands of the sun were nurturing Nature into her finest growth. To celebrate the New Year some of the older girls, as was the tradition, put on a play. This year's theme was 'Forgetfulness & Remembrance.'

Two of the older girls played both the king and the queen. Teresa recognized that their gymnastics teacher Anna played the role of the queen. Another girl, with dark hair tied back, played the king. A narrator announced them as a just and respected royal couple who lived in a far-away realm of perfection. They had a wonderful son and daughter and they all lived together in happiness. One day the king called his children before him and said: 'The time has come, as it does for all. You are to travel far, far away, to another land and fulfil a mission. You are to seek, find, and bring back a precious spice.' So the two children dressed as travellers in disguise and were led to a strange land whose inhabitants, they were told, almost all lived a dark existence. The narrator described how such was the effect of the strange land that the two children lost touch with each other, wandering as if asleep. From time to time they thought they saw phantoms, resemblances of their own country and faint glimpses of the spice. The two girls playing the royal children wandered around the patio looking lost and bewildered. Their faces were pale and ghost-like, and their actions jerky. It was all very believable. Then their behaviour changed. They began to perk up and dance around and have fun. It was as if they had forgotten everything of their mission. It was then shown and narrated that the king and queen received word about their children's condition, which worried them. They called forth a trusted servant, a wise woman, and gave her the following message to transmit to their children: 'Remember your mission, awaken from your dream, and remain together.' The trusted wise woman went forth into the far-away realm to seek out the lost children. On finding them she delivered the message, and upon receiving this message the children awoke from their reverie. With the help of their wise friend and guide they dared the challenges and perils that stood before them and the spice. Once they had obtained the spice they then by its magic were able to return once again to their realm of peace and perfection - there to remain in increased happiness for evermore.

After the performance was over everyone clapped and cheered. In the early afternoon sunshine it had stood out as a wondrous show. Then when the buffet was finished the tables were cleared away and La Madre's familiar chair was brought outside to the patio. Shortly, La Madre appeared looking relaxed, draped in a simple white woollen shawl, and stepping out onto the patio she walked past the girls and seated herself next to a small table with a pot of steaming tea. 'I shall make this brief so you dear ones won't catch a chill. I know what you're all thinking. Its wonderful sunshine – how could we catch a chill? And yet sometimes even the light of the sun can deceive, if we are not attentive. And it's about being attentive that I wish to speak of. You all enjoyed this year's play, did you not?'

All the girls nodded attentively.

'Good – me too! And I know your clever little minds have already figured out that the children in the play are us. We are the children – for now and always. It is said that before we enter into this world our souls drink deeply from the River of Forgetfulness, so that when we are born we remember nothing of our mission. Some even say that as soon as we pop our little baby heads into the world an angel taps us – boing! – on top of the head and makes us forget everything. Well, well, well – if it's not an angel it's a river, or something else in that regard. But people in this world have forgotten that we all came here with a mission.' La Madre paused to take a sip of her tea. She carefully looked around the patio, seemingly making note of everyone.

Teresa felt, or knew, that it was a deliberate pause.

'And,' she continued, 'our mission right now is to help all those who have forgotten to remember again. They need the *special ingredient* that is the spice.'

The day ended well. Everyone was happy and content, if somewhat pensive. Things had been quiet after La Madre's talk, as if she had triggered some trekking into the interior worlds.

Tibia was sat up in bed reading one of her books. Alicia was sitting on Abigail's bed combing her friend's long blonde hair. And Teresa was lying on her back, eyes closed and resting, her mind traversing amongst the stars.

Tibia looked up from her book. 'Do you remember anything, Teresa?'

Teresa kept her eyes closed. Tibia repeated the question, although she knew that Teresa had heard the first time.

'Sometimes…,' whispered Teresa softly. 'Like they are my memories, but they're not. Maybe when you make peace with many of your earlier memories they then make room for these other ones to enter…do you remember how it was under the earth?'

Tibia closed her book and stared into space. 'Yeah…,' she said after a long pause, and that was all. That was all that needed to be said.

Alicia rested her head on the back of Abigail's shoulders. A silence fell over the room and gently caressed each occupant with its fingers of remembrance.

CHAPTER SEVENTEEN

~ Where there is no harmony there is no possibility for engaging with the essential ~

The early months of a new year are always the most exhaustive. People become restless, impatient for the first buds of spring to announce their arrival. The shorter days and darker evenings take their toll upon physical bodies, upon all too fragile emotions. Few are immune from the wisps of ennui that lounge around the days of mist and chill.

Any place where people gather, whether in a fixed location or on the road, conditions arise for human behaviour to be observed. Life is more than just a hall of mirrors; it is a sparklehorse of splintered fragments each showing an image of the whole. Even passive tempers fray when grazed enough times.

Madam Aisha purportedly witnessed the confrontation as she crossed the patio from one wing of the building to another. Two of the older girls were arguing, with bullet-words that were nasty and made wounds where before there were none. It was a day for shadows. They crept disingenuously across the stone walls, and through the cracks like usurpers. There were tensions in the eating hall too. Stony glances and fixed stares accompanied the lines of hungry stomachs.

It was Saturday when an irregular meeting was called for all girls to attend, despite their ages. It was held in the very same eating hall, with tables pushed back and chairs arranged in rows. Around the room stood the Madams like beacons, ready to relay their signals to far off places, beyond the reach of shadows. La Madre entered the hall accompanied by her trusty companion Madam Aisha. She gently lowered herself into her grand chair and waited for the teapot to be brought. There was a silence of expectation in the hall that itself was heavy.

La Madre took a sip of her tea. Then she spoke for all ears to hear.

'It is a privilege to be here. Do not forget this, or ever take it lightly. To be in this group, and to have this opportunity to work together, is truly a privilege. We are each working towards something that is greater than any one of us. In this life we need gifts. Without gifts we are unable to move forward. Being here together is one of those gifts, and the Azafran Home for Girls benefits from this gift of energy. Yet everything comes with its price – there is no free lunch, as they say. And one of those prices is the need for harmony. Where there is no harmony there is no possibility for engaging with the essential. It is as simple – and as important – as that. We could not exist here in this place, and do what we need to do, without this special harmony. It allows us to do our work, and to help others. Remember clearly that what we do here is not for ourselves. We cannot - must not - be selfish. Disrupting the harmony we have established here is a selfish act. Harmony is what brings things together into a correct alignment, and which facilitates our aim here. It is a word that is heard often, and yet it is of the utmost importance. It is both very powerful and also of great fragility. It lies inside each one of us, and also operates between us. Dear ones, if there is no harmony we can do almost nothing. Trust in this. Trust in yourselves.'

La Madre finished her cup of tea and left. Another seed had been planted within each heart of conscience.

CHAPTER EIGHTEEN

~ The genuine expression of a truth takes no fixed form ~

The other three had already been called in. Teresa was going to be the last. She didn't get to see the girls afterwards so she had no idea how it went for them. Teresa had been kept waiting separately until Madam Aisha came and gently called her in.

It was the same room as before; only this time Teresa sensed a different atmosphere. On the small table sat the crystal bowl. On the other side of the table was seated La Madre. She gave a soft smile as Teresa entered, and motioned for the young girl to sit down.

'I say to you the same as I said to your friends. This is not a test. Tests are for those expecting certain criteria. Here, we look for recognition. Everything you do is in recognition of where *you* are. Each time you recognize yourself you assist in your own preparation. Now, take your time – you know what to do.'

'If I'm not ready now, I won't be ready in five minutes.' Teresa spoke quietly in a matter-of-fact voice. Then without hesitation she leaned forward and lifted the crystal lid from the bowl and placed it on the table beside it. She then lifted up the lid again and replaced it upon the bowl.

La Madre nodded as she acknowledged the silence. 'You have the good sense not to delude yourself. Everyone has their own ways. Some need their time. Some need pomegranates.'
Teresa pulled a face of surprise. La Madre gave a little laugh as she unexpectedly stood up and walked over to the window. Teresa noticed how gracefully and nimbly she moved. She too stood and followed the older lady to the light of the window.
'There is much light here, where we are. Light is good for our work. Our home here is not a majestic cathedral, but it still lets in good light.'
'I like it here. I've always liked it here. Home is where the heart is, right?'

'The heart, yes, and much more. Yet that certainly is a good start. How are your readings studies going?'

Teresa wasn't expecting that question. 'Mm, interesting. I didn't understand why we all had to read science-fiction at first. It seemed odd…but now I enjoy it. It makes me think.'

'Exactly.' La Madre gave Teresa a cheeky wink. 'And now?'

'Now, well, it's less fun since we started reading some of the classics. At the moment we're reading the big, long inferno book by Dante. It's heavy going.'

La Madre appeared to nod in approval. 'Yes, now you are reading different material. Yet consider what links all these themes together: Dante's journey through the underworld to find his Beatrice; Odysseus returning home to Penelope under the guidance of Athena; Theseus following Ariadne's thread through the Cretan labyrinth; and the medieval quest for the Holy Grail.'

'Yes, these journeys really get my mind going. I still have images in my head after closing the book.'

'And that is why we read such books. Teresa, the next step for the saffron collector is to have greater access to the world of the creative imagination. When we sow the saffron seed, we do so between two worlds. We do not operate only in one world, one reality; if we did so the flower would not hold any special properties. The seed is *infused* with its properties that come from another realm of forms – a purer realm. The saffron collector acts as the bridge for this infusion to occur.'

There was a silence. Teresa looked out of the window onto the fields that stretched away into the distance. Then she turned to La Madre who was standing beside her. 'And so the creative imagination is the first step in combining these worlds'?

La Madre nodded. 'Now, I want to give you something. Come.' She moved away and walked into an adjoining room, with Teresa following.

Teresa had never been in this room before. It was one of La Madre's private quarters. It was a narrow room, and it felt warm. Even the cold stones of the walls and floor gave Teresa a feeling of warmth. The room also had a feeling of being low. Maybe it was because all the furniture was low to the ground. A low two-shelf bookcase that was full of books ran along one wall. Placed along the top of the bookcase were odd looking carved bowls, some with chains. On the wall opposite to the one with the bookcase there hung a bright tapestry with intricate patterns. At the end of the narrow room there were cushions placed upon the floor. It was a simple room. No doubt, thought Teresa, it had a simple purpose too.

La Madre went over to the bookcase and selected a thin

book. Giving it to Teresa she said 'here, read this. Practice the exercises, and work with the visualization.' She then reached out and placed her hands around Teresa's face. La Madre came close and whispered something into her ear.

Tibia waved to Teresa from the other side of the glass-panelled door. Teresa was happy to see her best friend, and quickly approached and entered into one of the side yards. Tibia embraced Teresa and gave her a happy kiss on the cheek.

'Well. Why such a happy you?' asked Teresa with a laugh.

'I did it! I did it, of course.'

Teresa hesitated, and then it dawned on her. 'Ah, yes, of course. You did the crystal bowl thing.'

'*Mais oui, bien sûr,*' replied Tibia with a pout. Both girls laughed.

'Don't let La Madre see you, or hear you, doing that!'

Tibia stuck out her tongue and Teresa couldn't resist a giggle.

'And then?' Teresa was thinking that Tibia was also given a book to study.

'Well…and then I was given some new duties to start on…'

'Which?' asked Teresa a little surprised.

'More gardening!' said Tibia with a laugh. She then pointed

down to where she had been working, at the small garden next to the yard. Teresa had not seen the trowel, or noticed that Tibia was holding a pair of gloves in her hands. 'And she also whispered something to me.' Tibia came close to Teresa and brought her mouth up to her ear, almost touching. 'The genuine expression of a truth takes no fixed form.'

Tibia stepped back and looked across at Teresa. 'And you? You did the crystal lid thing, right?'
Teresa nodded and gave a wink.
'And anything else?

Teresa shrugged. 'Just a book.'

CHAPTER NINETEEN

~ We are here to compel change upon others ~

It was the day of the race. All the girls lined up in their outdoor clothes for the Annual Azafran Cross-Country Race. The morning had begun with a low mist that smothered the fields. There were three routes according to the three age categories: 7-12; 13-18; and 18 plus. Any girls younger than seven were not permitted to participate. Or, as La Madre liked to say – *it all depends on time and pomegranates.*

The race was always exhausting. It pushed the girls to make extra physical efforts; such efforts that they were not normally used to. And the girls knew that there was no prize for the winner - for there was no winner, and no losers. There were only participants. Participation was the golden thread that joined them all together.

And afterwards there would be a fiesta of sandwiches, cakes, and special treats. The girls would be tired, and yet after the race this tiredness would become transformed into an incredible energy. The race day fiesta was always an energetic affair, with the girls discussing the details of their race - the difficult parts, the fun parts, whether they ran with or against the other girls, and the rest. As the race was about participation rather than winning, just how each girl participated was the true matter at hand. It was all a question of attitude and etiquette.

The Azafran Home for Girls was a microcosm for the wider world. The girls soon learned that when they reached an older age they would most likely leave and re-enter the world. Only that where and when they did not know. It usually happened around the age of twenty-five, although some girls stayed longer; and some girls left unexpectedly early. And the very few stayed on forever, becoming Madams and running the home. There were often rumours amongst the girls, especially the older girls. Who would be leaving next? Where would they be sent to? It was an odd thing that no one was ever around to share the news. As soon as a girl was chosen and asked to leave, they left immediately and did not speak again with their friends. Yet the one thing that all the older girls agreed upon was that they were very definitely sent somewhere. One didn't just walk out one day and wander. And so the girls knew that somewhere out there in the world there were saffron collectors, in places unsuspected, occupied with things people were unlikely ever to know.

In the evening of the race day all the girls would come together for a talk from La Madre. It was one of the few occasions where La Madre would speak to everyone collectively. It was one of her annual talks, where a theme was always selected. The energy of the day would create a buzz amongst all the girls. It was also a day that marked the beginning of spring. And that was enough to bring excitement into the hearts of winter-weary girls.

It had turned out to be a mild evening, and so the talk was arranged to be outside in the main practice yard. On this occasion it was difficult for many girls to hide their enthusiasm. They were almost restless as they waited for the arrival of La Madre.

As ever, La Madre knew how to utilize the art of timing. She often appeared when least expected, and delayed her appearance when most anticipated. Patience, perhaps, was the theme. When at last the collective restless energy of the gathering had subsided into acceptance, La Madre appeared and calmly seated herself in her chair. She waited patiently for her pot of tea to be brought; then sipped from her cup, eyeing the faces before her. A sparkle glistened in her eyes.

'Today officially marks the first day of spring. You could also say it marks the true beginning of the year. It is significant in that it marks the time in Nature when seeds are sown, and the annual transformation in the natural world gets under way. The natural world has her rhythms and we have ours. She has her ways and we have ours. And those things which are seemingly in opposition are often working in harmony. Behind the appearance of contradictions often lies the greater truth of conciliation. This harmony, this working in unison, creates another force – the force of transformation, which I wish to speak on today. Transformation is not a passive path. It does not ask for solitude or a life of tranquillity – it asks you to be warriors in the inner sense. If you wish for release from obligation and work, then seek your sanctuary elsewhere. With me, you are contagious agents of a new force. We are dealing with the present condition of humanity and the planet, and there are forces hostile to our aims. Such forces never willingly let go of their power; not unless they are compelled to. We are here to compel that change. We are here to compel change upon others. When we work with the spice we connect with it. We communicate and become in correspondence with it.

Likewise, the saffron flower, during its time of growth, has been in correspondence with certain forces from nature, from the sun, and from the planets and the stars. All these influences are in a special mix within the saffron flower. And its spice, when mixed with the inner being of the *right* person, becomes an ingredient for transformation. There is the potential for correspondence between the spice and the saffron collector. This is a correspondence of the Angel Fire, the golden river within, which flows from the stars into us. It is an energy that radiates and animates us. One who deals with the saffron spice must make contact with their psychic being – that inner part of them that always has an influence on a person's outer personality, unbeknown to them. To cultivate the psychic being we need to be attentive to it – to listen to it with all genuine sincerity. It must exist every second of every minute within your worlds of creative imagination.'

Something within Teresa jolted when she heard that phrase. She recognized it immediately. Her senses seemed heightened, as if triggered to be more alert, more alive. She thought she could feel the prickle of energy around her, as if they were all within some vibrant fizzy field. Teresa sensed that they were in a protective energy, something so strong and yet almost unperceivable.

'If you run away from this world,' continued La Madre, 'and from your responsibilities within it, you leave open a space for adverse forces to rush in. Do not let them in! Likewise, do not oppose negative forces with weakness. It's like blowing on a flower - you only serve to further spread its seeds. Goodwill alone is not an effective force for transformation. A conscious intent and personal power is required, to be applied in the right way and when necessary. With a conscious intent you can deal with all the impacts and noise coming from the outside. It is a very physical work and can occupy the whole consciousness and conscious awareness of a person. A person must be transformed in order to correctly deal with processing and neutralizing external impacts. A transformed person is also more capable of working with the properties of transmission and dissemination. One transformed person can compel great change upon this planet according to necessity and function, whilst a million untransformed people can do nothing. Compel the change within you, and step into your destiny.'

La Madre looked up as the first twinkle of stars began to appear. 'And may a star guide you upon your way.'

It was time to go indoors.

CHAPTER TWENTY

*~ Each of us here goes into the world as a book that
doesn't need to be read aloud ~*

Madam Pym eyed the girls from the other side of the kitchen. Her rounded face emanating her attention like a searchlight. It was clean-up duty day for some of the girls, which included Teresa and her roommates. As they washed up the pots and pans in the kitchen several of the girls joked amongst themselves. Teresa also noticed that Alicia and Abigail were in bright moods that morning. But no voice was more noticeable than that of Madam Pym's. Her deep tones kept a control over proceedings, yet as soon as anyone looked over they would see the kindly, sympathetic face of the grey-haired keeper of the kitchens. Her large voice was accompanied by observant, twinkling eyes and a mouth that seemed endlessly on the verge of breaking into a radiant smile.

Tibia nudged an elbow into Teresa's ribs. 'Hey, let's sneak out later and go through the paths. We can climb up in our favourite tree. Maybe we'll be lucky and get a rain storm!'
Teresa nudged her friend back playfully. 'You are something, Tibia. You'll get us into trouble. You're like the little devil that sits on my shoulder.'
Tibia giggled. 'Better me than some fat ogre smelling of garlic.'
'What are you two whispering about? You look like two hens plotting a farm escape.' Madam Pym came over and tapped her fingers on the kitchen work surface. 'Mm, nice and clean. You two do more than cackle like hens, you actually scrub!'
'More than just a pretty face, Madam Pym,' said Tibia with a grin.
'Aye, and that's important, dear one. The face is for the world. But here, we work with what's below.
'So why is kitchen duty part of working with what's below?'
Madam Pym patted Tibia on the shoulder. 'You should ask your friend about that.' Tibia looked across at Teresa who was standing on the other side of Madam Pym.
Teresa nodded in recognition. 'Discipline.'

Madam Pym smiled approvingly. 'She remembers. Yes, there is no discipline within if there is none without.'

Tibia betrayed the slightest of frowns.

'I know, my dear. There are some things you may not like, yet we are not here solely for our own sweet desires.'

'The more time I am here the less clear things become.'

'You are here, dear. You are *here*. It's always about where *we* are. Everything has to come through us – has to work through us. La Madre says that each of us here goes into the world as a book that doesn't need to be read aloud. The wisdom is not in the pages of a book but in our presence. And people will read us in many varied ways.' Madam Pym gave Tibia a sympathetic look. 'And that is why one day you, and others like you, must return to the world – to be amongst it.'

Tibia's face had turned into a calm seriousness. 'I actually don't mind cleaning the kitchens.'

'I know, my dear. I know.'

The evening encounter was unexpected. It was not very often that the older girls frequented the corridors where Teresa and her friends were situated. And yet that evening as Teresa was walking towards her dormitory she saw Anna coming towards her. Anna was tall and slender, and perfectly suited to be their gymnastics teacher. She had taught Teresa and the others for many years. She was almost like a big sister, except that the relations between Anna and her students were always respectful rather than sisterly.

Teresa smiled at Anna as they were about to cross paths. Yet Anna stopped instead of walking on.

'Evening, Teresa.'

'Hello, Anna. A pleasant surprise to see you.'

'Pleasant, yes, although not a surprise from my part.'

Teresa tilted her head almost imperceptibly as she considered the remark. 'You were expecting to meet me?'

'On this occasion, most definitely. Come, walk with me a little.'

Anna walked slowly down the corridor with Teresa beside her, two girls of different ages and different heights. They came to a large bay window which had a cushioned bench beneath it. Anna sat down and waited for Teresa to join her.

'You don't see it yet, but look closely.'

Teresa followed the direction of Anna's gaze. She was looking across at the tiled wall. There were many tiled walls within the large building, along with tapestries and pictures.

'Sometimes we fail to see those things which are right in front of our eyes.'

Teresa looked again at the coloured tiles arranged in geometric design.

'This particular wall is made from four thousand and ninety-six individual pieces. And yet it still does not easily reveal its function. Soften your focus.'

Teresa let her eyes go lazy and her focus blurred. After a short time an image began to form through the colours of the tiles. A pattern came together that transmitted an image…and then an understanding. A sense emerged, whole and complete. And then Teresa understood. She turned to Anna and gazed at her. She knew Anna had understood the same message, and that this was what she had wanted to convey to her too.

Anna nodded. 'Yes. When you have the understanding there is no need to put it into words. Words only distort the transmission and lose some of the meaning. Soon you will be one of the saffron collectors, and then you too will be charged with the transmission. Our aim is to transmit without distortion. That is, not to allow ourselves to distort what comes through us. It is very hard not to get in the way of the understanding, but that is our work. That is what we must do. The transmission must be seeded in specific locations at a specific time. These are not arbitrary choices. True transmission is more like a science, just like in a laboratory a correct heat is applied to the correct mixture of elements. Yet our laboratory is the world.'

'And our elements are…'

'Yes. Exactly.' Anna didn't let Teresa finish her sentence. There was no need anyway. Both had understood.

Anna turned to Teresa and pulled in close. She brought her head to touch Teresa's and for a brief moment they stayed like that, with foreheads touching. Then Anna slowly pulled away.

'There is always the connection. Without it there would be no life. To be cut off from the contact is to be cut off from the energy of transformation. We are all connected, only that most people do not realize this. Without the transmission they would wither like a flower without sun or rain. These things are our responsibility.'

Anna stood up and straightened her dress. 'We shall not be seeing each other again. I am now twenty-five years old and, like others before me and those still to come, I am to leave. Spring will soon be here. We remain, as always, connected.'

Teresa remained sitting on the bench as Anna walked out of view.

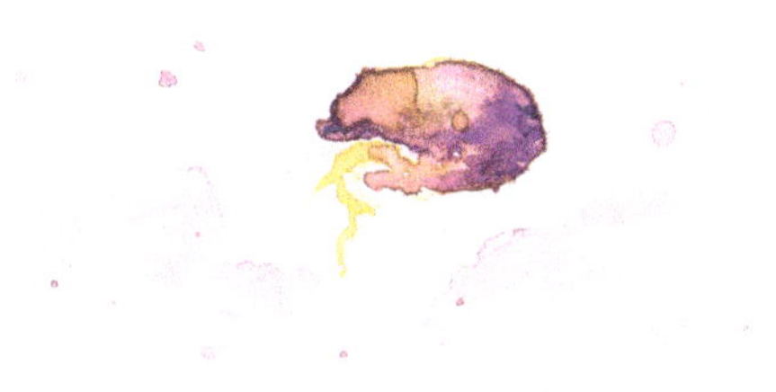

CHAPTER TWENTY - ONE

~ You are the spice of the saffron ~

The spring renewal arrived on time. The light had a stronger intensity. It was sharper and crisper. Sixteen girls were sitting in a circle around La Madre in one of the smaller patios. The sound of running water from a fountain filled the morning air. A few birds could be heard chirping as they flittered past in playful pairs. A ray of light fell across La Madre's lap as she sat in her chair, her eyes closed and her face serene. She then took a long look at all the young faces seated before her.

'Springtime is a special time. It is made even more special when I have my girls seated before me. You shall become the next round of saffron collectors. Yet before one collects one must first seed. There is nothing to collect if nothing has been seeded. Next month you shall plant the bulbs. And in autumn they will be harvested. Between now and autumn we will need to come together regularly. You are now ready to sow the seeds, yet you are not ready for harvesting. I shall make you prepared for the harvest. This is what La Madre does.'

Madam Aisha entered the patio with a large teapot and one teacup on a tray. Behind her came Madam Pym with an even larger tray filled with sixteen teacups. La Madre deftly took the teapot and without a fuss filled each of the sixteen cups with the hot tea. The last cup she filled was her own.

Teresa brought the cup to her nose and smelled the hot perfume. She recognized immediately the scent of jasmine. She closed her eyes and took a sip. Her entire body sensed the warm communion. Everyone drank in silence, as if acknowledging an unspoken baptism between them. Yet deep within Teresa, in her own unspoken place, she knew she had already been baptised by La Madre.

When the cups were empty Madam Pym collected them and quietly left. Her movements gave the indication that she had done this many times, over many years, and everything was as it should be.

All eyes and hearts returned to La Madre. 'We are all made of light. The deeper the darkness in the world the more light that is needed. Some of this light is provided by the sun, and is reflected here upon the earth. Most people know of only this light. It has its uses, yet it is not the greater light. There is another light which comes from deep within us – a light that shines from a different star. It is this light of which there is a greater need. Like fish in the deep oceans where light does not reach, there are places where this greater light must be taken. There is a responsibility to bring this greater light into the world, into our everyday life. The unfolding begins deep within us like a seed – it is part of the hidden feminine presence which nourishes and maintains the unseen patterns of our world. When we can see this, we also see that everything in life is connected to this. We can allow ourselves to be engulfed by the Great Mystery. And then, once we have been engulfed, we have to be willing to be dismantled, again and again, so that we finally go beyond who we think we are. Then shall we have the ability to be both present and absent. To be present in this world, yet also able to shift into *another place*, allows one to tune into what needs to be done here in the everyday. It is a connection which has maintained the world since humankind first placed her feet upon the earth's soil. And what we do can only be done through a very special, a very unique, feminine *quality*. It is this quality of connection which is the power that weaves together our hopes and days. It is a way, a path, for us that requires sincerity. If you are not truly sincere – with yourself and with *Her* – then you can't make it. There will be obstacles that keep presenting themselves, and only sincerity will clear the way. Through the vessel of sincerity flows love.'

A different energy had arrived that day and infused the patio where all the girls were seated. It had collected them all together and fused them into one. Looking back at that moment, Teresa knew that everything had really begun in that instant, with that talk. And Teresa recalled La Madre's final words that day…

'Each one of you will now become the spice of the saffron. The secret, if there is one, is this: the spice and you are one and the same. So it has always been, and so it shall always be. This is the path of the saffron collector. Welcome to the new springtime of your lives. Welcome home.'

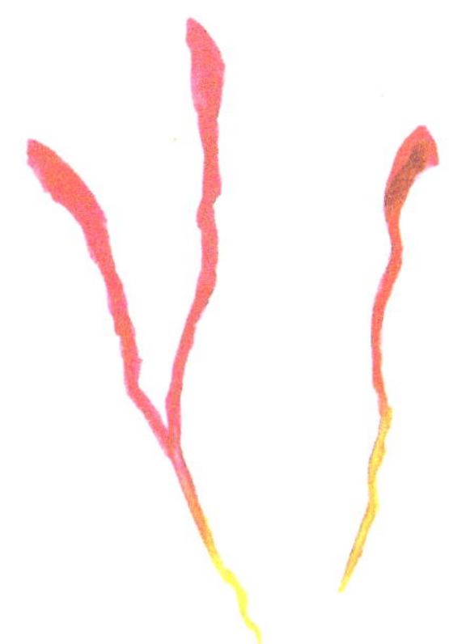

SPICE

The saffron spice blends things together – it adds a special something to what already exists to create something else – something different from what was before. The spice is a catalyser. It knows how to take what was before and to re-blend.

CHAPTER TWENTY - TWO

~ If you work just for yourself, you limit yourself ~

Teresa plunged her hands deep into the soil. She carefully lifted the saffron bulbs into their bed, fifteen centimetres below the topsoil. Again she plunged her hands into the soil. Ten centimetres further on she placed another saffron bulb into its bed of soil. Each one was under her care. Each tiny plant became an extension of her self. The sun was waiting overhead to supply the needed warmth. Teresa thought back to the time when La Madre had also planted her beneath the earth. Her guidance had been like the warmth of the sun. Teresa now knew why it had been done. It was all part of the process to develop the connection, the *communication,* with the saffron. Unless one has had the experience, one cannot truly know. Teresa smiled to herself as she remembered one of La Madre's anecdotes… 'A man fell off the roof of his house one day, and his wife came running out – "oh, I shall call you a doctor immediately." "No! Don't call me a doctor," replied the man. "Call me someone who's fallen off the roof before!"'

Teresa chuckled quietly to herself. Yes, she thought, that's exactly how it is.

The sixteen girls were out in the fields, each assigned to their particular plant beds. There were many saffron bulbs to plant. *Many to seed for such little spice.* The saffron crocus, small lilac-coloured flowers, were pretty to look at. Yet their real function was to be the mothering vessels for the intimate spice. Something larger contains the smaller – the greater is but the outward face of the essence. *People like the pretty lilac flowers, but seldom are they drawn to the spice.* The words of La Madre resounded in her head as Teresa planted the saffron bulbs. She planted them one by one, one after the other, many of them; each different, each the same. It was hard work, out in the fields since earliest dawn. And yet Teresa recognized that she wanted to be nowhere else at that time. She was in the right place, at the right time, doing the right thing. And this recognition – this *knowing* – infused her whole being. Then she remembered another of La Madre's phrases: true freedom is having no choice. And now it made sense, finally.

The day was long, and the body felt the pressures of physical exertion. Teresa also felt exhilarated with the work, and she noticed this too in the other girls. The body had been pushed to a state of exhilaration through exhaustion. There had been little talk throughout the day; only the necessity of rest stops and some food. Soon after dark the troupe of girls were ready for a shower and their beds. There was an unspoken feeling of communion between them. It was as if each girl sensed the state of the others. Indeed, they were sharing the same experience.

Come together, exist through the group. The first thing to remember is that your own self-interests are not the goal. If you work just for yourself, you limit yourself. You must allow yourself to be used by that which has no name and yet knows all names… the words flowed through Teresa's mind as she lay down upon her bed to sleep.

Teresa saw La Madre in her dreams. As she slept she saw herself walking down an unknown street. She didn't feel lost, although she did not know where she was or where she was going. Teresa turned to look in a shop window and there was La Madre, standing before her and smiling. 'Oh, La Madre, it's so good to see you!' La Madre came close and clasped both of Teresa's hands in her own, and squeezed them tight. And then they began to walk together in this way, both of their hands clasped together. 'La Madre, I know this is a dream. But I need to ask you – am I doing enough? Am I going forward?' La Madre continued to squeeze tightly Teresa's hands. Her presence and energy was so intimate, so warm. 'Do you really need to ask me that? You have the answers…look for the roots.'

It was dark when Teresa opened her eyes. Dawn had not yet risen. Day was still night, and yet now the night was into day. Teresa lay quietly in bed, sensing a slight vibration throughout her body. Something within her body was humming…like a low buzz. Teresa closed her eyes and spoke internally to herself.

By the time she opened her eyes there was already movement in the room. The other girls were getting ready for an early start. Another day of planting lay ahead of them. It was the second day. There would be three days of planting. Three days of intense physical labour.

In those three days there was no sign of La Madre. The girls were left to concentrate on their work. Yet La Madre was present in all their thoughts, in each moment of concentration and attention. In those days the mind was working just as much as the body.

Consistency and persistence…ignorance is not cured by adopting the easiest methods…

Teresa placed herself back into a moment where one evening, after gymnastics class, she was sitting with her friends listening to a talk from La Madre. Teresa could remember well the words that La Madre spoke. Many times Teresa had re-visited this memory, these words, their meaning, as they touched her deeply. They had become a part of her…

'…Each flower has its unique essence and quality. A flower may have the essence of timidity, joy, wealth, melancholy, majesty, or dignity. The saffron flower has a very special essence, and you must find it. *If you can find the true essence of the saffron flower you must pass this on to me. If you do this, a great secret shall be revealed.* You can know the essence of a flower by observing how its colour flows. For example, yellow going towards green symbolizes a "mind essence" in the flower. The beauty of flowers is that they do not deceive, do not try to lie or mislead others. And best of all, they do not delude themselves. They are exactly what they are. They literally display their essence for all to see – for us, the birds, bees, trees, and all of Nature. They are exactly what they are. They live in their essence. From this we could learn much. People rebel against their essential nature, whether they know it or not. People may say a thousand things – or only one thing – and yet in each spoken moment they move away from the essential. Who am I? How can I know myself more and become a better person? How do I develop?…what do these things mean to the everyday person? They are abstract concepts, at best wishful thinking. And yet they are essential questions. They are the steps one takes to move toward knowing one's essence. Unless this is done, everything else we do in life is only a fragment…a fragment of who we truly are. Observe the flowers, and learn from them.'

Teresa plunged her hands again into the soil, into the soul. She so deeply wished to understand the essence of the saffron flower. She imagined one day she would whisper those words into La Madre's ear.

CHAPTER TWENTY - THREE

*~ The act of giving has benefit in accordance with the
consciousness of the giver ~*

The girls rested for a day after the last of the planting was finished. Despite the physical exertion there was a sense of vibrant energy amongst the group. The group of sixteen girls was comprised of four dormitories, one of them being the room which Teresa shared with Tibia, Alicia, and Abigail. There was a new found closeness now between the four dormitories, as if the planting had brought them together in an unspoken way. They felt that they had shared something unique; something unsaid yet understood... something beyond the daily sharing of their bathroom.

A day after resting and all the girls were called to a

meeting with La Madre. They were too many to fit into her private quarters so they were asked to come to a study room adjacent to the library. When they arrived they saw that La Madre's chair, with her now familiar table and teapot, was already prepared.

'Thank you all for coming. I know you must all be tired after your work in the fields. And yet, I'm sure you still have enough energy within you.' La Madre gave only the slightest of smiles, yet it was obvious to Teresa that she knew exactly how they felt. Teresa wondered too whether she could feel the energy of vibrancy amongst them. Surely, it must be evident?

'As you can all sense,' continued La Madre, 'we have entered a new phase now. Previously, we would hold our gatherings on Tuesdays and Thursdays after gymnastics class. This shall no longer be the case. Those gatherings are now for those behind you, filling the shoes you yourselves once filled. Yet the wave moves along the shore, and brings us to where we are now. We have planted, and now what lies ahead for you is to prepare for the harvest. We are in spring, and the harvest comes in autumn. There is little time, and much to process, if you are to become saffron collectors this year. So now we begin a series of what I call the 'Spice Meetings.' I apologize for the title, I couldn't think of anything better to call them so I stuck with what I know. Why complicate matters further?' This time La Madre did give a smile; an obvious one for all to see. Teresa observed carefully. She was watching not only the words and behaviour of La Madre but also the sense of her presence. It all felt like every act was carefully orchestrated. Nothing was being left to chance. Even the smiles, thought Teresa, were calculated at the precise moment.

La Madre paused in her speaking and glanced carefully around the room. She looked at everybody and acknowledged them. Everybody, that is, except Teresa. Again, deliberate. It was as if she was saying to Teresa – 'Watch me. Observe me.' This sense was as strong within her as the rays of a summer's day – as certain as there was the moon above them, thought Teresa.

'We are all children of the moon.'

Teresa's heart almost skipped. There it was again – that connection...

'And as children of the moon we shall gather together, all of us here, at each new moon and full moon. And as you shall come to know, the saffron collector is a child of the lunar consciousness. This is something we should be acutely aware of. The saffron collector not only collects but, more importantly, also gives. The act of giving has benefit in accordance with the consciousness of the giver. And the consciousness we work with is the principle behind the hidden relationships through which the visible and invisible dimensions of life are connected with each other. It is a sacred principle – a fertile energy – which regenerates through Nature and through our human cultures. It is an instinctual force, a life-giving force, that is nurturing, compassionate, beneficent; but also it can be a powerful force of destruction within Nature. The essence of the spice is a sacred, living transmission with no religious building, formal structure, or earthly institution - it is transmitted through the hearts and minds of people. And when people are gathered together, or in correspondence and communion, they are connected to the spice essence which ensouls the world. The saffron collector not only observes but also participates in this living force, applying it consciously to the world around them. The essence of the spice, the living transmission, can only communicate through those individuals who have become receptive to its presence. *We* are receptive – we are lunar – and this energy will manifest in the ways we think, feel, and imagine. It will filter into our actions, our lives, and into all our ways of being. And it shall spread and nurture our cultures – and yet it all begins with a single drop.' La Madre paused for a minute of silence. 'This has been our first Spice Meeting. And yes, we are under a new moon.'

The scent of jasmine tea drifted through the room.

CHAPTER TWENTY - FOUR

~ Our aim is to transmit without distortion ~

Teresa adjusted well to her new daily routines and responsibilities. They were now part of the 'older girls,' or whatever they wished to call themselves. There was no name. It was just that *things* had changed now. Many of their earlier responsibilities, such as breakfast preparation and kitchen cleaning, had been handed down to the younger girls who had arrived later. It all seemed very natural, just like the seasonal cycles. One season passed over to another, and everything continued in its place. Teresa and Tibia had now been assigned to library duties whilst Alicia and Abigail had been given 'Reception' duties, which meant dealing with all aspects of the orphanage's relations with the wider community. This included receiving guests, arranging visits for new girls, and dealing with local liaisons. On hearing the news of their allocations Tibia frowned and looked over at Teresa. She felt she had been given the more boring of the duties, on account of Teresa often dragging them both to the library on numerous occasions. Teresa, for her part, knew that such allocations were carefully thought over.

'I guess we have a predilection for the library.' Teresa tilted her head in the way that often made Tibia sigh.

'Well, I guess you've just got a pre-dilec, or whatever, for eating dictionaries!'

Tibia pouted as Teresa winked at her. It was a friendship that was harmonious through being different.

The sixteen girls, now often referred to by La Madre as the saffron collectors, were assigned new reading and study schedules. Finished were the classical novels, which many of the girls felt were often too long-winded anyway. Now they were reading a mixture of modern psychology, social science, history, natural sciences, and philosophy. Yet, as they had later found out, they were not all reading the same books. Each girl had been prescribed a different set of books to read. Similar, but different. And then there were the other texts too, not found in the regular books but delivered as privately printed booklets. These consisted of…well…as Teresa would say, they were a 'different way of looking at life and things.'

Teresa and Tibia were under the guidance and supervision of Madam Morag, who was the Head Librarian. Or rather, as Tibia used to joke, the 'Head Book.' Madam Morag kept a low-profile in comparison to the other Madams in the Azafran Home. She was small, thin, and somewhat delicate. She tied her greying hair back into a bun and was quite unassuming. She spoke softly in a lilting and often whispery voice. She only spoke when she needed to, and always economically. Her small green eyes were gentle yet observant. Teresa liked her instantly.

Madam Morag had showed them how the library functioned and all the duties they had to perform.
'Of course,' said Madam Morag as she finished her opening introduction, 'this is not a library in the sense of just storing static books. Oh no, here we maintain the tradition of transmission.'

Both girls looked at Madam Morag, not sure what she was getting at. The older lady walked into a back room and the two new library assistants followed her. The room smelled of age and time. Teresa sensed that it was a place that bridged different ages, like a living conduit. Along the stone walls were wooden bookcases stacked high to the ceiling.
'Wood, stone, paper. Paper wraps rock, scissors cuts paper,' said Madam Morag as she made the now famous

corresponding hand movements. 'But thoughts? Understanding? Knowledge? These things cut through everything because their existence transcends the material objects which serve as their vessel. Words too are vessels; perhaps the most misunderstood vessels in our history. And yet there are many things more powerful than words. Thoughts, for example, are more powerful than words. Words can elicit thoughts, and vice versa, but when thoughts are projected as words their power becomes diluted. Words are dangerous because they are open to misunderstanding, abuse, and deliberate manipulation. And yet this world we find ourselves in places more emphasis upon the spoken word. It is harder to perceive the quality of a person's thoughts, yet much more necessary to do so. It is necessary for us here to make very deliberate and careful use of books. And so, the library is anything other than a boring place to be.' At these final words Madam Morag gave a brief glance over to Tibia, who tried to look innocent. She then ran her fingers gently along the spines of several books before choosing one to pick out. She handed the slim volume to Teresa.

Teresa saw the title, nodded, and handed it back to Madam Morag. She had understood the message.

'Sometimes the sole function of the book is transmitted through its title. Or there may be just one phrase within the whole of the book that is operative and serves the function. A book may be the book of the book, or it may be for the reader to know exactly how to know. Books are the vehicle for words, yet their true function is as carriers for thoughts. And particular books operate as *specific carriers* for intentional thought patterns. Likewise, they may serve to induce specific thought patterns, or to dismantle current thought patterns already inculcated in a person's mind. If something is not capable of being transmitted, then what is its purpose?'

'Books are like flowers.' Teresa spoke the words quietly under her breath. But she had not spoken quietly enough.

Madam Morag did not respond but silently showed the girls where the drawers were that held the keys to the locked shelves. She then led them into the records office and showed them how to register all incoming and outgoing books.

'Oh, yes, well, there are some boring aspects too.'

Tibia smiled. She also liked Madam Morag. 'Why didn't we have duties with you before, Madam Morag? We've never seen much of you before.'

The older lady nodded slightly. 'Yes, that's because I don't work with the younger girls. It's only after they've learnt some of their breakfast duties do they cross my path.' She almost smiled.

As they were about to leave the office Madam Morag gave each girl a handmade bookmark. Upon the bookmark was a dried pressed flower – a saffron flower.

'The transmission in which we participate requires of us that whilst we may act independently we do not become attached to our individual effort. Individual effort is only one of many means of action. There are forces that act upon us and those that act through us; and these forces have greater power if we allow our collaboration. Our aim is to transmit without distortion - make this *your* individual effort.'

As the two girls left the library after their induction they both felt a slight buzzing in their bodies. Neither of them said anything at the time.

At meal times all the girls at the Azafran Home would eat together – from the youngest five-year olds to the oldest girls. Teresa and the other girls in her age group had now begun to form a strengthening bond. They naturally began to eat together, all sixteen of them, which had not happened before. Another girl the same age as Teresa – Beatrice – was part of another dormitory and yet recently the two girls had taken more notice of each other. As if quite naturally Beatrice began talking to Teresa during mealtimes. She was very matter-of-fact, almost brisk in manner, and yet Teresa noticed she was very observant. Beatrice was quite tall for her age, and had a well-built, physically strong body. Teresa had noticed from their gymnastics classes that she had been the most physically dominant amongst them. Her black shoulder-length hair gave her face a strong, but not harsh, aspect. Beatrice was accompanied at most times by her roommate Simone. Simone was very different to Beatrice, as she was shorter, and with a rounded face that was framed by a somewhat unkempt auburn hair. She was a year younger than the rest of them and she had a physique that was slightly rotund. Yet the main thing that contrasted Simone against Beatrice was the fact that she almost constantly wore a smile on her face, whilst her more serious roommate kept a sober appearance.

Teresa had noticed all through lunch that something was on Beatrice's mind. Finally, Teresa looked across the table and raised her eyebrows, giving Beatrice her cue.

'There's something different here now – don't you feel it?'

'I feel many things different,' replied Teresa. 'Are you referring to something specific?'

'I mean here, in this dining hall. It's not the same as before. It's almost as if we've been disconnected in some way. How do you feel about the rest of the people here, besides us sixteen?'

Teresa knew that Beatrice was right. She had sensed it herself, and the feeling had only grown inside of her since the days of the planting. It was as if they had shifted further away from the others around them, especially from the younger girls. And here in the dining hall it had become more apparent. They were all gathered together, and yet the sensation of detachment was so strong.

'Yes, you're right. I've felt it too. We've become apart from the rest. Maybe that's part of becoming a saffron collector?' Simone and Tibia were listening to the conversation.

'Well, it would explain why the older girls always seemed so aloof to us!' The comment sounded ironic, yet Beatrice's face remained deadpan.

'Well, wherever it is we're going we're certainly further along now,' added Tibia.

'Yes, everything has become much more intense now.' Teresa looked at her friends and saw that they all agreed.

'Even the reading is more intense, whooh!' Simone shook her head with a mock look of exasperation.

Teresa smiled. 'Sure is. It's full on now. Intense all the way…'

CHAPTER TWENTY - FIVE

~ Goodness lies deep within all things and can be found,
if sought ~

It was a crisp spring morning and the dew was still upon the ground. Soon the girls would need to enter the fields to water the saffron plants. The saffron beds were open to the incoming rays of the sun and so they needed adequate water. They were bedded in a well-drained silty soil, and since the land did not keep a hold onto its water the girls had to be attentive.

As Teresa was coming in from the fields with the other girls she noticed Madam Aisha standing by one of the outer doors. The older madam motioned to her to come over. La Madre, she was told, wanted to see Teresa and her roommates. She would be waiting in her private quarters. They were to go to her immediately after washing up. This was unexpected. Teresa looked around for the rest of her roommates.

Teresa noticed immediately the difference. There was no pot of tea prepared for La Madre on her side table. Otherwise everything else in her private quarters was the same as usual. In that case, thought Teresa, this shall not be a long visit.

La Madre stood up to greet the four girls – Alicia, Abigail, Tibia, and Teresa. She then motioned for them to come closer. Not a word had been spoken since the girls entered. The small group stood close together. Still, La Madre gathered them even closer until they were all huddled around each other. The five women, young and old, now formed a small, tight circle. They brought their heads together until they touched, and La Madre placed her arms around the group. Each of them remained silent, sharing the communal embrace. Time ceased – or at least that's how the girls would later describe it. Finally, La Madre removed her arms and the girls stepped back, disbanding the circle.

'I have released an invisible golden thread, like a flower stamen, from my heart to yours. Like collecting saffron, we now prepare to collect our own thoughts. We are to remain, now and always, in contact. We shall meet regularly, here, with just the four of you.'

'And the other Spice Meetings, with the other girls?' asked Abigail.

'They shall continue. Meetings require other meetings; no girls, or groups of girls, are alike. These smaller meetings are to develop *our* connection.'

'And the other dormitories have their meetings too?'

La Madre looked over at Alicia and smiled.

'My dear, do not concern yourself with the others. We should not make use of comparison, the same as you would not compare the different ingredients of a dish. We have gone beyond the general now.'

Teresa realized the truth in La Madre's words. For many years the only contact they had with La Madre were in the general Tuesday and Thursday gatherings where all the girls could participate if they wished to.

'Thank you for your time and attention,' said Teresa softly. 'We realize how much of your time we girls must take up.'

La Madre gave a gentle smile. 'That is the whole point though, isn't it? You are *all* my time – all of you together, and individually. What I can do with a large group cannot be done with a smaller one. And what can be said to a group of teenagers cannot be said to a group of seven-year olds. Saffron is not planted in winter; neither is it harvested in spring. The sun doesn't rain and the moon does not provide its own light. Everything *gives* according to what it can, and thus we must approach each and all according to its capacity and essential nature. This is not voodoo, dear ones; it is the science of the heart.'

'And the golden thread? You mentioned it a moment ago.'

La Madre laughed quietly, showing a more relaxed side to herself.

'Ah, Tibia, ever the curious one!'

Tibia blushed. Yet it was apparent she was still waiting for an answer.

'Curiously determined too,' continued La Madre. 'The invisible golden thread is what has been planted in your hearts. It was seeded from the very first day you arrived here. From your first meeting with me I planted the seed within you and it has been growing every day. Each of you here will one day bring your part of the thread into the whole tapestry. From that moment we contribute and participate in the whole design, knowing of its patterns. We are then connected in ways not visible to others. We take this with us when – or *if* – we go out into the world. Our connection to this golden thread reminds us constantly that goodness lies deep within all things and can be found, if sought.'

Teresa felt a shiver run through her, and wondered if the others had felt it too.

It was odd, or perhaps uncanny, yet after that meeting in La Madre's room a *different* relationship grew strong and evident between all the sixteen girls. Teresa felt it without doubt, and it reminded her of what Beatrice had spoken of recently when in the dining hall. It was if there was a different type of energy moving through them now. Only that Teresa didn't wish to think of it as 'energy' for that was too crude, too simplistic. In fact, she didn't wish to give it any name or wording at all. It was a sensation, an experience – a knowing. And that was something which Teresa well knew could not be communicated through the normal ways.

'You're pondering again,' said Tibia as she climbed into bed. Teresa pulled the white laced handkerchief from out of her long hair and placed it in her bedside drawer, as she did every night.

'Mm,' she murmured, half-listening.

'You always do that too – mmmm.' Tibia gave an exaggerated murmur and giggled. Teresa smiled over at Tibia and a deep fondness for her friend rose up within her.

'I know,' said Teresa. 'Goodnight.'

CHAPTER TWENTY-SIX

~ A gift is but a tool whose use each person
must choose ~

The full moon had come around and, as is the way of the saffron, the sixteen girls were gathered in the presence of La Madre. There was a respectful silence of communion, each girl knowing that they had come together for something that bound them beyond the cords of friendship.

It wasn't a prayer. It was more like an inward connection with the golden thread – a knot that tied to each heart differently. When the silence had finished, La Madre took a sip from her teacup and began to speak.

'People are many things that they themselves do not know. They can be blind and not know it because they are blinded by a light that makes them look away. Through this blindness many people only know themselves by the name they have been given and which they wear through life. If pushed, they would find it difficult to truly distinguish themselves from others who bear similar conditioned attitudes and opinions. And yet such people hide themselves from this realization. The shock of knowing this would greatly disturb their mental and emotional balance. And so they continue to identify and individualize themselves through the given name they bear. Such people, when asked *who they are,* reply with their occupation. It's a most unsettling question for them, and so they can only answer this by their work function or their given name. Yet *who* they actually are remains a lifelong mystery to them. And this is a condition common to many humans, and gives us some mild concern.'

La Madre paused to take another sip of her tea. Some girls shuffled in their seats. Otherwise the study room remained still.

'Reason, dear reason – both a blessing and a curse for the

human being. A gift is but a tool whose use each person must choose. Generally speaking, reason is considered to be the peak of human thinking. For the world at large it represents the best of human thought. And yet reason is like a pair of dry eyes that cannot cry – it lacks the feeling of the innermost part of us. Life is not about the skeleton, the dry bones of a human life – it is much more. It is about everything that makes the flesh of a human being. Reason does not compel us to *seek,* nor can it provide a 'reason' why a person should seek for something beyond the ken of accepted human knowledge. Reason often hides the realization that some people are actually seeking without recognizing this within themselves. They do not see the patterns of a search – a *longing* – that is woven through their daily lives. Unfortunately, it is often the case that a tragedy or catastrophe is the trigger that opens a person to recognizing their condition and compels them to seek answers. We live with questions all our lives, and yet often fail to notice them or to awake them from their slumber within us. How many of us have honestly and truly asked ourselves the question – "why am I here?"'

La Madre paused again and looked around the room at the sixteen faces and thirty-two eyes.

'Have you not wondered,' she continued, 'why events have

turned out this way – why you ended up here?'
Again, silence fell over the study room.

'Yes, of course we wonder.' Teresa's voice broke the silence and the tension suddenly eased. 'It would be odd if we didn't wonder about such things. Yet personally speaking, rather than inventing an answer to keep me satisfied I'd prefer to wait until I arrive at the place where I actually *know* such answers.'

Tibia tickled Teresa in the ribs. She was sure glad that someone had said something. And more than that, she was glad it had been Teresa – another reason to be proud of her best friend.

La Madre nodded, and then continued. 'Curiosity and pride are just two of the features that pervade our world. And relatively speaking, these are the lesser of our concerns. In fact, one of the strongest features that the world suffers from is not an active aspect but a passive one. It is the aspect of inertia. The everyday world is awash with inertia – it is a widespread and prevalent energy that we must be conscious of and careful about. It is necessary to guard ourselves against inertia. It is an energy – a state – that people all too easily fall into. It sweeps up the masses and swirls them around. Like I have said – we go *forward*; we do not do 'around.' The type of energy you choose to identify with will mark more than your personality – it will mark how your future unfolds. Such paths are not set in stone, as many wish to believe. All paths are open and adapt to circumstances, decisions, and opportunities taken as well as those missed. And to simply recognize inertia is not enough – a person needs to guard against it.'

La Madre took another sip of tea.
'How is inertia recognized?' This time it was Beatrice who spoke up.
La Madre pressed her hands together as she considered the question. 'Sometimes we recognize things by their effects. And, more often than we may realize, such effects are contrary to their cause. In terms of inertia the effects are often manifested as excess. Society lacks discipline in dealing with such facets of inertia as disenchantment, and the unfortunate cultural disease of boredom. Disenchantment and boredom can become a dangerous energy – it can suck a person dry until they become like shrivelled fruit.' La Madre smiled to herself. 'That is one of the reasons – and only one, mind you - why life always requires the saffron spice. Our spice is a wondrous antidote to the disharmonious charms of disenchantment.' La Madre rocked back in her chair and allowed herself a quiet laugh. Although none of the girls could quite understand just what the joke was. Later, Tibia

confessed to Teresa that La Madre suffered from the cultural disease of 'private-joke-a-mania.' But that, said Tibia, was just a private joke between the two of them, and winked.

'Do you think it's true?'

The girls in the dormitory all looked across at Abigail.

'What's true?' asked Alicia.

'What La Madre said about disharmony beginning with humanity, and then filtering out into, what did she say – all our social streams?'

'Well, why not?'

'It just seems such a shame, that's all. Why would we want to create disharmony?' Abigail sat on her bed in her nightgown and fiddled with her long blonde hair.

'I don't think she means that humanity consciously and wilfully creates disharmony,' replied Teresa. 'That's just the thing; most of what occurs through us is unrecognized. A lot of what goes on in the world is through our ignorance rather than our deliberate intentions.'

'That's right,' added Tibia. 'Nature doesn't act through reason; it has its own sort of nature-natural instinct. That's why La Madre said that disharmony and disequilibrium are unnatural to it.' Tibia looked over at Teresa to see if she had said it right.

'Yeah, it seems that a lot of the disharmony in the world is some kind of subconscious manifestation of humanity's inner lack, or disquiet.' Teresa slipped into bed, yet not before taking off her prized possession, the white lace handkerchief.

Abigail sighed. 'I wonder when we shall be entering into the wide wild world out there?'

'Soon enough,' replied Teresa as she rolled over onto her pillow. 'Last one in bed turns out the lights.'

CHAPTER TWENTY - SEVEN

*~ The sacred is not only in the stillness inside of you but
also in all the spaces in-between ~*

Teresa had spoken of her idea to Madam Aisha who had then passed it on to La Madre. Apparently La Madre thought it was a wonderful idea and gave permission for the game to go ahead.

Teresa had thought out the game rules in a general way but first wished to see how things played out. The best rules, she thought, were those that were flexible. So one summer morning after breakfast and before the sun rose too high and the rays became too strong, Teresa assembled the fifteen other girls onto the field. Also joining them were Madams

Pym, Celia and Morag, as well as a couple of the older girls. It was to be the first game of *Saffron Softball* to be played at the Azafran Home for Girls. Teresa didn't yet know it but it was to become a historical moment in the annals of the Azafran Home.

Each team was composed of eight players and, as Teresa described it, the game was a kind of cricket-with-softball.

'Why not just play cricket?' one of the assembled girls had asked.

'Because the rules of cricket are fixed. And besides, they don't hit you with the ball in cricket.'

All the girls looked at Teresa wide-eyed.

'Well, it is a *softball* after all – it's not going to hurt anyone.' Teresa then explained the rules, as far as she knew them. The pitch would be like cricket, with batting at one end. The bat was a soft sponge bat shaped like a baseball bat that the Home had managed to acquire. Each team member would have three tries to hit the ball. On the third try they would have to run whether they had made a hit or not. The objective was to reach the other side of the straight running pitch. That would constitute one run, and one point. If they made a return run they would score another point. Meanwhile the other team not batting would act as fielders. Their role was to collect the ball and either return it to the bowler, who would be standing inside the running pitch, or to get the person out directly. To get a person out you had to catch the ball before it hit the ground or for the ball to make contact between the runner and the ball. Usually this meant throwing the ball at the person, which was difficult in mid-run, or to throw it to the person standing at the end of the pitch who would tap you with it before the runner could cross the line. A scorer – in this case one of the Madams – would be standing at each end of the pitch to take score: one point for every time a runner crossed the line. If the person batting made a good hit they would be able to keep running, maybe three or four pitch lengths, until the ball was returned. There would be an umpire, or referee, observing the whole game. In this first game it was Madam Morag who took that role. The referee would note down the runs provided by each scorer at each end of the pitch. They would also be the time-keeper. Each side had twenty minutes before the roles would be reversed and those batting would enter the field to defend against the other team. In total the game would last forty minutes and the team with the most points would be the winner. Those were the basic rules of the game. And then there was the flexible scoring part. This was the bit which could change during each game according to how it was played. The umpire-referee would also score each team according to how they played the game – that is, according to their behaviour, attitude, and team management. If the team showed good sportsmanship toward their opponent; if they didn't throw down the bat when running; if they behaved calmly; if they were organized and orderly, and so on and so on. All these factors could add points to a team, and it was the role of the umpire to decide these. And no one would know how they were calculated. Likewise, points could be taken away for disorderly play; bad attitude or mood; disagreement during the game; messy organization…and so on. And so, it wasn't just about how many runs each team scored; it was also about *how* you scored them. And the umpire's decision was final. As Teresa explained – 'a game is more than a bat and a run.'

And so on that bright summer morning the first game of *Saffron Softball* was played at the Azafran Home for Girls. It was a lot of fun but also there was a focus on discipline that forced the girls to be aware of the game they played. Teresa was team captain of her side and Beatrice was the other team captain: two sides, two dormitories on each side. It was also exhausting and took more exertion than many of the girls had anticipated. Alicia and Abigail were both thoroughly worn out, whilst Tibia turned out to be a sporty whiz. Yet after the game was finally over, and all the official points and 'flexible points' were added together, one team had to emerge the winner. It was close, but not close enough. Everyone cheered and gave congratulatory hugs.

Madam Morag walked over to Teresa. 'I'm sorry your team didn't win. Especially since it was the opening game and it was your game, after all.'

Teresa wiped the sweat from her face. 'That's okay. I don't mind losing if we lost fairly. It means we have more to look forward to when we do win. Besides, it's not my game anyway – it's for everyone.'

Tibia came running over. 'Fun-tastic! When do we play again? How was it, Madam Morag?'

'Well, an interesting first play. I have a feeling a new era has just arrived to our home.' Madam Morag gave the two girls a wink and moved away.

There was excitement along the dormitory corridor that evening. All the girls were speaking about the game, and analyzing their game play. Everyone unanimously declared *Saffron Softball* a success and all were eager to play the next game. In the communal bathroom the girls were sharing ideas amongst their team mates, and deciding how to improve on their performance for the next game.

Tibia came running excitedly into the dormitory where her roommates were preparing for bed.

'They've named themselves the Spice Girls!'

Alicia and Abigail looked at Tibia with blank expressions.

'The other team…,' said Tibia without pausing for breath. 'Beatrice has just declared it now in the bathroom. Her team has called themselves the Spice Girls, and she says no one else can have the name. We need a name for our team now!'

The other girls all looked over at Teresa, who was sitting quietly in bed reading a book.

'The Spice Girls!' said Abigail with a huff. 'That's a terrible name. No one in their right mind would ever call themselves that!'

'Cliché,' added Alicia.

'Well?' asked Tibia.

Teresa finally looked up from her book. 'This too shall pass.'

Tibia frowned. She had hoped for a more dynamic name for the team.

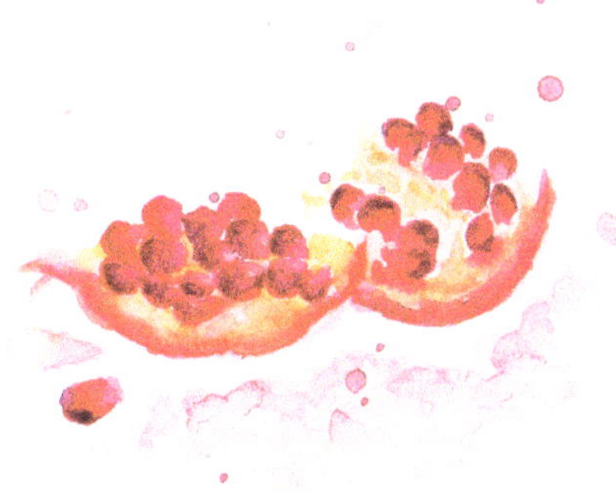

CHAPTER TWENTY - EIGHT

~ Seek your own speechless communion with the centre
inside of you ~

The new moon had come around and, as is the way of the saffron, the sixteen girls were gathered again in the presence of La Madre. The intervening weeks had been full with intense learning. Teresa, for some undisclosed reason, had been asked to familiarize herself with the musical scale. Although it had seemed an odd request at first Teresa soon found the study much more agreeable than the natural sciences. Teresa was quietly going through the do-re-mi-fa-so-la-si-do of the musical scale in her head when La Madre began speaking.

'People's general sense of what freedom means has been deformed. It has become twisted into a caricature of personal desires and wants, which then become translated as needs. True freedom is none of these things, and stands apart from these reckless musings which have infiltrated the mass social mind of humanity. If you feel lonely amidst the presence of others, this is a sign that you are not yet fully connected within – you must endeavour to seek your own speechless communion with the centre inside of you – a private source that you can trust. True communion will be your freedom. Then you can be alone without ever feeling lonely. To be alone with the lonely and to feel connected is part of the freedom that the spice gives us. Without this connection you are unable to make use of the power of silence. Without the golden thread, if I gave you silence - what would you do with it? How would *you* benefit, and help others to benefit, from the silence? The power of silence is a gift. We can dress ourselves with this beautiful gift and walk amongst the world as a true warrior of the heart. Yet you must learn first to befriend your silence – make it your companion. Your companion is also your personal centre. It is the place deep within you where you are always sincere. It is the place that knows you better than you know yourself, and from which you cannot hide nor lie. When a person is in contact with this sincere centre, they can perceive the impersonal psyche behind all things in the world. From such a centre one can enter into communion with the living energy that pervades our world – one can be in communication with the intelligence of the saffron. This is true freedom.'

La Madre took a sip of her tea, and paused.

'Will communication with the intelligence of the saffron help us to communicate with other intelligences?' asked one of the girls.

La Madre nodded. 'We must learn how human thoughts affect the physical and psychic world. Human thoughts can, when manifested in certain ranges, pass directly from individuals and groups into the world, without the need for vocalization. The effect of this is often much greater than is realized for the sole reason that it passes largely unperceived by ordinary perception. Positive thoughts, as well as destructive ones, can create both intended and unintended physical and psychic consequences. We can be enhanced or weakened by such thought frequencies. Part of the communication that we enter into is to observe and regulate such frequencies.'

Suddenly Teresa's do-re-mi's took on a new significance. *Of course, the power of music, of sound…it is a frequency, a vibration.*

A voice inside Teresa had instantly become alive and alert.

'If you start from very little – first giving away what little you do know – you shall reach a finer form of understanding that only creative imagination knows. In the way of the saffron there is no false compulsion - no compelling force from outside that can oblige you to our way. It is right to make effort, yet you lose focus if you then artificially force yourself. You can gain from making the right effort, but lose from undue force. Do not hold back, or be afraid, from making right *effort*. Those who are afraid, are afraid everywhere – those who have faith and trust inside themselves shall be safe, wherever they go. There is only one genuine compulsion, and it pulls from within to the without. Trust in this, and trust the instinct that speaks to you, as the saffron speaks to the spice.'

During the next pause Simone gestured that she wished to ask a question. La Madre nodded for her to speak.

'How strong are the forces that compel us from without? Do they – can they – interfere with our special communication?' 'They are strong, and they play a game. They try to give you *their* mind and convince you that it is actually your mind. The world is, in a sense, a mind game – and it is imperative we know *whose* mind we are operating through. Much of the world, unbeknownst to it, is operating through…well, we can call it a *foreign mind*. If we do not recognize this – this mind game - then it is imposed upon us from the outside. And this can cause great difficulties. In an ideal world everyone would recognize the game – but this is not within reach yet. So, I say to you, you must take responsibility for your energy, and for your frequency of communication. If you feel something, or feel connected to some energy, then you should acknowledge this, and be a representative for your own source of energy. You may wish to appear timid on the outside – yet do not be timid within yourself. Do not shy away from this source of energetic communication within *you*. Avoid those things which only serve to destabilize you or detract you from your work. Do not try to appease those forces that work against you – move around them. After all, when you enter a field of saffron flowers do you not choose to be near the beautiful saffron rather than the weeds?'

The next day Teresa and her roommates arrived to meet with La Madre in her private quarters. To begin the meeting La Madre brought all the girls close together in a circle and again placed her hands around them as their heads touched.

It's the golden thread – it must be woven between us. This is the way of the saffron.

'The summer is moving on,' said La Madre as she walked over to the window. 'The harvest is fast approaching. It is always an intense time for the first year of the saffron collectors. How are your studies going?'

The four girls each in turn talked about their studies and how, more or less, they spent their days. As the other girls were speaking Teresa observed La Madre, and how she was listening and responding to them. It soon dawned on Teresa that La Madre wasn't so much interested in what they were saying. It was if she was observing something else…or monitoring something within each girl. Teresa sensed that La Madre, through these meetings, was also examining the manner of their presence – their *being*. La Madre was listening and responding to something else within each girl, and the words, the talk, was just a smokescreen – a camouflage.

'Yes, Teresa, there is concealment in all outer appearances. Is this what you were asking?'
Teresa looked up, startled out of her reverie. And yet she hadn't asked a question – had she?'

CHAPTER TWENTY - NINE

~Behind the appearance of contradictions often lies the greater truth of conciliation~

The next week had come around and, as is the way of the saffron collectors, a second game of *Saffron Softball* was arranged. The same two teams, with the same girls in each, were preparing to play against each other another time. And it was a game with the same rules, and the same 'flexible' way of earning or losing points.

Beatrice approached Teresa with a wide smile on her face.

'We're the Spice Girls y'know.'

'Yeah, we know that.'

'And you – what's your team called?'

Teresa turned her head to the side as if thinking. It was a deliberate gesture, and an empty one for Teresa already knew the name she had chosen for the team. 'We are the "Blue Roses",' she declared.

Beatrice pulled a funny face. 'The Blue Roses? What kind of a name is that? It has nothing to do with the saffron, or what we do here!'

Teresa nodded as if agreeing. 'Sure. Yet what we appear to do and what we actually do are two different things.'

Beatrice laughed. 'Anyway, smarty, there's no such things as natural blue roses. They don't occur in Nature – they're just made-up, invented!'

'Exactly.' Teresa smiled and walked back to her team – the Blue Roses.

'Weird,' mumbled Beatrice under her breath.

The game was fun. This time the players had gained from the experience of the first game. They were quicker to recognize how each girl batted, and their preference of swing. Some girls preferred to swing the ball to the left, and others to the right. Some batters liked to lob the ball high in the air, which meant there was the possibility for a direct catch which would take the player out of the game. Other players preferred to hit the ball down against the ground so they could not be caught out. This meant that the ball would travel less distance but they would need to be caught out by being touched by the ball.

Many of the girls loved throwing the ball at a runner in the hope that it would hit them. Few balls ever did find their mark, and the other fielders would have to go running to retrieve the ball. Teresa kept her team in an orderly line as they waited to bat. They had been told, or rather warned, not to throw down the bat before running. It had to be calmly dropped. And Teresa had also told the Blue Roses to clap in appreciation each time a player was knocked out of the game, regardless of which side they belonged to. 'Support all players,' she had said. 'We don't take sides – not in the bigger game.'

Under the summer rays of a gentle blue-sky morning the girls of the Azafran Home for Girls played their new game. And with each minute they played they accumulated greater experience.

Beatrice put her arm around Teresa and gave her a playful hug. Simone and Tibia laughed whilst Alicia and Abigail looked on, bemused.

'Congratulations, you did it this time – you won!'

'Yeah, the Blue Roses rock,' said Tibia with a laugh.

'Spice Girls gonna get you next time, you bunch of flowers!' Simone also gave Teresa a winner's hug.

'Thanks all, it was a fun game.' Teresa finished washing up in the bathroom and returned to her dormitory.

Tibia, Abigail, and Alicia all came over to sit on Teresa's bed.

'They're going to come back strong,' said Alicia. 'The Spice Girls will want to win next time.'

'Sure. And they may win.'

'What do you mean by that, Teresa?' Tibia frowned, and the out-of-keeping expression made Teresa laugh.

'It's okay. The Spice Girls are physically stronger than us. They have more sporty players.'

'We have sporty players too!' protested Abigail.

'Yes, we do. But it's not about brute strength. *Saffron Softball* has more levels than that. We won today because we were more disciplined. We didn't throw the ball around all the time trying to hit the other players out. That was a waste of time – you nearly always miss! No, we had more structure in our game. We made a plan and we stuck to it. All of us! We worked as a team today – as one big blue rose – whereas the Spice Girls played as a bunch of girls. There's no point in winning if we cannot act and move together, as one.'

Remember the golden thread, it weaves us all together

Teresa closed her eyes, feeling sleepy, as she felt something tug at her - within her.

CHAPTER THIRTY

*~ Make your reality a dream, not your dreams into
reality ~*

The dawn's early light fell across the stone walls of the old majestic building. Teresa was leaving the meditation room and returning along one of the ground floor corridors when a ray of light caught her eye through one of the windows. The sudden and unexpected flash momentarily blinded her. She stopped and looked out at the glaring sunlight, muttering under her breath the lines from one of her favourite poems – *Busy old fool, unruly sun, why dost thou thus, through windows, and through curtains call on us?*

It was then that she spotted the figure of La Madre standing outside in the patio yard by the fountain.

Something within her demeanour, her presence, beckoned to Teresa. The young girl stepped outside into the early, crisp morning air. She approached La Madre, who had still not turned her head to acknowledge her. Finally, as she stood beside the older lady, La Madre turned her head and gave the slightest of smiles.

'La Madre?'

'My dear child, bring your face here so I may wash it a little.'

Teresa stepped toward the fountain and bent her head forward. She felt the gentle touch of La Madre's hands upon the back of her head as they pressed upon her. Teresa's head entered the cold, crisp water…

…she brought her head up and took a gasp of air as the sunlight hit her in the eye and blinded her. Teresa wiped the water away from her face and saw the stream flowing at her feet. Her heart almost stopped. This was not where she was a moment ago…then laughter filled the air. Teresa turned around to see that she was in a meadow and nearby was what looked to be a picnic gathering.

'Come on, sis!'

An arm grabbed hold of Teresa and pulled her up. Teresa looked at the girl's face, and her eyes widened.

'Tibia – you are here too!'

Tibia laughed. 'Of course, silly – we're all here! Come.'

Tibia led Teresa by the arm over to the picnic place where others were eating. As they approached Teresa began to make out their faces – and they looked familiar.

'Tibia, what are we doing here?'

Tibia laughed in a playful way. 'We're having a picnic, of course, like we always do! Did the water wash your brain away?'

Teresa felt odd, out of place, as they arrived at where the others were seated on a rug laid out upon the grass. Now that she was close Teresa could recognize the faces without doubt.

'La Madre?'

'Ah, there you are, Teresa. I'm glad your sister managed to bring you back for something to eat. Come, sit down.'

Teresa turned to look at Tibia. My sister? Teresa felt disorientated, as if she had just walked into the wrong scene of a play.

'But La Madre, why are we here?'

The older lady laughed gently. 'My dear, what's with the strange name? Mother is fine; I don't need any strange affectations. Now come and eat, before you starve your brain. Your cousins Alicia and Abigail have joined us today.'

Mother…cousins? Teresa sat down and across from her were two other girls, both with blonde hair. They smiled over at Teresa and munched on their sandwiches.

'I think you fell asleep, Teresa, over there by the stream. Did you have a nice dream?'

'Yes, mother,' replied Teresa faintly.

Teresa recognized them all, but the scene was different. Here, they were a family. But this was not her world. Or had the world of the saffron collectors only been a glimpse of some other world she longed to visit and to be a part of? Had her desire to be a part of some grander life pushed her fantasies into a daydream?

Time remained as if fixed. Teresa returned home with her new family and everyone treated Teresa as if they had all been together for all their lives.

The years passed and Teresa and her sister grew up into fine young ladies. Eventually, both Tibia and Teresa got married off and started their own families. Teresa bore two boys to her husband and her mother eventually was granted her wish of becoming a grandmother. Sadly, Teresa's father was no longer around to take the role of grandfather. Yet Teresa was content with her family, and of the love of her husband.

 For many years after that special day of the picnic Teresa continued to think back on her dream of the saffron collectors. Yet after time that was all it became – a dream she had dreamt by a spring stream. It had been so vivid, so real. And yet it had vanished as soon as another reality took over.

Teresa had wanted so much to continue her life as a collector of the spice. It had given meaning to her. Although a dream, it had actually meant something. And so Teresa never forgot about that special dream; and of living at the Azafran Home for Girls. Although the memory became less vivid over the years, she could never completely forget it. Often, when alone away from the attention and responsibility of her family, she would think back at her time at the mysterious orphanage. Yet such dreamlike thoughts increasingly became a fantasy as other events took over Teresa's life. Her mother passed away at a ripe old age, and a large gap opened up in her life. Her two boys eventually moved out of the house and began their own lives.

Time passed, and the everyday mundane became the only reality Teresa knew. When Teresa's oldest son was killed in a farming accident the news hit her hard. It was a shock from which she never fully recovered. Nor did the marriage survive the rupture of this heartbreaking event. Teresa finally divorced her husband and for a time went to live with her sister, Tibia. Teresa came to feel incredibly lonely, and she felt too that somehow her life had managed to slip away from her. What happened to all those dreams as a young girl? All the amazing things she had wanted to do? Hadn't she wanted to change the world? These were the naïve dreams of a little girl, and the world had become too big and too demanding for her young dreams to survive. Teresa felt a large hole within her, and it was there dwelling everyday. She had wanted to make her dreams a reality instead of her reality into a dream.

One evening before bed Teresa looked at her face in the bathroom mirror. An old, sad face reflected back at her. Tears started to stream from her eyes. Was this it? Was this her life? Teresa, once a girl full of joy and play, could no longer laugh. She could not even laugh at herself. The tears poured down her cheeks. Teresa opened the taps of the wash basin and filled her hands full of the cold, crisp water which she splashed onto her face…

CHAPTER THIRTY - ONE

*~ The world binds us to it – we each of us belong to the
world, yet each in our different ways ~*

er head was pulled back by the gentle hand of La Madre. The fresh, cold water of the fountain dripped from her face. There in the early morning sun stood Teresa, gasping, her heart pounding.

'How long was my head under the water?' Teresa shook the water from her wet face.

'About two seconds,' replied La Madre.

'Two seconds and a lifetime.' Teresa felt dizzy.

La Madre nodded at Teresa's remark. 'We belong to the world in different ways, my child. And there are endless threads that we can bind ourselves with.'

Teresa stood in silence, not knowing what to say, or even how to say it. She had felt a lifetime of experience in two seconds. And she had also lived a lifetime without knowing the spice. Teresa had experienced what it truly felt like to have a hole inside of her. And she never wanted to experience that world again.

The study room was again filled with the sixteen girls. La Madre was leading another one of her 'spice meetings' and the girls were eager to listen to her words.

The shuffling stopped as La Madre walked into the room. She looked around before sitting down. 'Ah, we've had another full moon,' she said before reaching for her cup of tea. 'Today I wish to touch upon attention and responsibility, similar to what we talked about in our last meeting. I trust you have all been considering what we discussed previously?'

All sixteen girls nodded attentively. La Madre smiled; she sensed the sudden shift in energy as everyone in the room consciously tried to be attentive and present. 'It's amazing what a gentle reminder can do,' she said softly almost under her breath. She took another sip of tea and let out a gentle sigh.

'Yes, well, we need to be attentive to the fact that the world binds us to it – we each of us belong to the world, yet each in our different ways.' La Madre threw a quick glance over to where Teresa sat, before continuing. 'We must learn what binds us, and what those binds are – whether they are chains, obligations, or willing service. What binds us can also be what nurtures us. In learning this, we find also our opportunities for freedom within the world, and of the ways which assist us, especially in our service. Nothing in this world is without its rhyme or reason. Through attention we can develop our individual presence. That is, we can create a point of energy that exists in this world, in this reality, and which can draw events around us. In this way we can *play* the game rather than being played. It is crucial that we develop our attention of presence. If not, we remain an unremarkable presence within the mass. We do not individualize ourselves.'

Here La Madre paused for her final words to sink in. Teresa had come to recognize that La Madre used her pauses as markers. They were intentional action, and not the random or automatic actions usually associated with the way people paused.

'There are fewer individuals upon this planet than is

generally thought,' continued La Madre. 'It takes development to become a unified individual. Until that time, a person is a reflection of a group – call it a group soul, as this term is more widely known. That is why so many people exhibit predictive and similar behaviour. If you observe – if you are attentive – you will recognize that there are many people who remind you of a particular *personal feature*. By knowing this range of features, we can know a great many people as they fit into these groupings. They are not yet fully individualised persons, and as such they are shallower as individuals. That is why some social institutions are so successful in their manipulations – they are not appealing to fully individualised persons. They appeal to a cluster of group minds, which are easier to persuade and – unfortunately – socially control. Individuality is the exception, not the rule. A very general feature is that people seek to forget. They may not realize this is what they are doing because they call it by another name. Through the seeking of pleasurable diversions and distractions, they are actually seeking to forget. Whereas *we* are here to remember – to not allow ourselves to forget. This is our duty. So many people live their lives on the surface – they are not attentive to life. They do not catch the fragrances of significance that brush past their senses. These people give flowers without real, inner intention. They put the saffron spice in their food without due thought or recognition. That is why there is such a great need for the saffron collectors – the spice taste comes as an important reminder. It is our responsibility to act upon the ignorance of others – we put the spices of significance and meaning into their food; we reach out to them and touch their worlds in ways unknown to them. We endow their lives with something special – we fragrance their world with just a pinch of essence. All this is done without the majority of the world knowing, or even suspecting. We are subtle; very subtle, my dears. Most people's attention is on the obvious, whereas we work with details. Our results are microscopic – they do not appear as grand gestures that set the world on fire. Yet enough microscopic events, with the right intention, will serve to create this grand fire that burns no one and yet alights all. Work with efficient gestures – not with illusionary grand, sweeping waves.'

La Madre made a big sweeping arch with her hand, and then rested into another pause.

Teresa was finding it especially difficult to remain attentive on what La Madre was saying. The girls, as always, took notes. Yet for Teresa her mind – her whole being – was still holding the fragments of memory from her other life, the one where she married and grew old without the spice – without true meaning. In some way or form, Teresa had actually crossed realities. And in that cross-over she had lived a life.

And eventually it had been a sad and painful one. She wondered how much of her body, of her physical memory, still retained this other life. Or was it only her mind playing the same recording over and over again?

The teacup clinked against its saucer. Teresa was jogged back into present attention.

'Our cosmic reality,' continued La Madre, 'is not the expression of mathematical equations. It is the play of poetic forces - and like a child it is intoxicated with love and wonder, and the joyful curiosity of adventure. And do you wish to know one of its secrets? It is delight...delight is the secret that lies hidden behind everything you see in this world. It's what gives the special flavour to the saffron spice – the unseen bubbles of delight that hold the spice molecules together. Delight plunged itself into every form so that it might encounter itself innumerably, over and over again – a glorious reunion without end - an infinite number of opportunities to encounter this delight. And yet in the middle of this delight are the forces of division and ignorance, that drive our world and make us see things in a different way. If we could gather all the delight together it would be the sweetest spice in the world, and a drop could be placed on everyone's tongue, and we could all share the experience of that taste without having to say a single word

– without having to spoil the experience by translating it into squiggles in the air that form words. And in each drop there would be a recognition of all the other drops, as if by tasting one you could taste them all. Now this would be beyond words – we would just *taste* and *know*.'

Another pause. This time one of the girls raised her hand.

'And how can a person find this delight?'
La Madre smiled. 'By not chasing desires as if they were delight, but by conquering fancies that the world throws at you.'

La Madre poured the last of the tea into her teacup.
'The saffron flower gladly gives its spice, playing its eternal game of love - as an eternal child in an eternal garden. You are like the spice of the saffron, my dears. And next time we shall discuss the spice. We only have two spice meetings remaining.'

La Madre stood up to leave.

CHAPTER THIRTY - TWO

*~ Where there is lack, there is need. It is our function to
recognize this need ~*

After study class the girls each went off to their respective work responsibilities. Teresa and Tibia entered the library to continue their duties, which was mostly re-organizing the books and putting them back on the shelves. Sometimes they had to deal with a specific request which meant a book hunt, which both girls enjoyed. The most boring part was the cataloguing, which was just 'paperwork,' or so Tibia would say with a sigh. However, time spent together in the library was also an opportunity for the two friends to work alongside each other, and in this way they got to know more about each other's manner.

Yet when they spoke it had to be in whispers.

Tibia gently nudged Teresa. 'Harvesting is getting closer. Don't you feel nervous?'

Teresa shrugged. 'Not really. More like a mix of being eager and apprehensive. We've waited a long time for this. But we must be ready, here.' Teresa pointed to the left side of her chest, and Tibia nodded.

'Do you think we'll be able to truly communicate with the saffron?'

Teresa placed a large, old book on the shelf under its catalogue number of 0786 and turned to look at her friend.

'We *have* to be able to communicate. The essence of the spice needs to come through us and into the world. You know we have to be this channel.'

Tibia pulled a face as if considering, or rather chewing, over something. Then she smiled. Tibia always seemed to know how to find a solution to the flurry of thoughts in her mind. Nothing kept her back for too long.

'You're so organized and disciplined, Teresa.'

At that moment Madam Morag came up to the two girls carrying a handful of books. 'Good organization and discipline are essential for a library to function well.' The older lady placed the books on the table in front of them alongside the others that needed re-shelving. 'And for much more besides the functioning of a library. What you do here is just the tip – *we* go down much deeper.'

Madam Morag gave both girls a friendly smile and left.

At the end of their shift Tibia made ready to leave, but Teresa said she wanted to stay to find some books for her personal reading.

'Fair enough, booksbody,' said Tibia as she gave Teresa a hug and left.

Teresa stood at the door to the office and gently tapped on its wooded frame.

'Come in,' came the reply.

Madam Morag looked up as Teresa stepped inside.

Teresa walked over to the other side of the office where Madam Morag was seated at her desk.

'I wondered if there was anything else I could help you with?' As she spoke Teresa felt as if the older lady's green eyes were penetrating through her.

Madam Morag smiled 'Well,' she said, 'I seem to have forgotten to close the door. Would you mind closing it for me?'

Teresa felt a sudden rush of tingling fill her stomach as she realized she had walked into the office leaving the door open. *How thoughtless of me!* Teresa recognized that the older lady was giving her a way to remedy the situation without the need for shaming.

'Yes, of course.' Teresa closed the door and came back to where she was standing. 'We only have a few weeks left, and I wanted to know if there was anything you needed me to do?' Teresa smiled, and waited.

'Anything that I need you to do? Or something that I would like for you to do? These two things are very different. What we want is most often not the same as what we need.' Madam Morag went back to her paperwork.

'What is need, then?' asked Teresa.

The Madam looked up. 'Where there is lack, there is need. It is our function to recognize this need. And it is our service to fill this need. That which we do is very exact and precise. You could say it is like a science. We work with correct quantities and with specific qualities. That is why the flowers are excellent carriers – and the saffron, of course, is the finest for us. Thank you, Teresa – I have no needs for now.'

'Thank you, Madam Morag.'

Teresa turned and quietly left the room. This time she made sure to close the door behind her.

The rest of the days passed with full hours. From early rise until bedtime all the girls on Teresa's floor were kept occupied with tasks to do. The sixteen girls were now accustomed to spending time together in close proximity despite their different duties. Some of those duties entailed working in the fields looking after the saffron flowers. This also involved pulling out the weeds which grew around the flowers. Teresa always liked this part; there was something about delving into the earth, into the rich soil, that nourished a part of her.

Teresa was pulling weeds when Beatrice came up to her, a watering can in her hand.

'Hey, Teresa, why is it I always see you down on your knees when you're here?'

Teresa looked up. 'Closer to the earth, I guess.'

'Are we not close enough already? We're out in these fields most days.'

'I don't think it's about distance – maybe it's more about touch.'

'Well, girl, I think we're already touching the flowers enough. Any more and we'll turn into fairies.'

'Too late, we're already fairies.' Teresa smiled.

Beatrice raised an inquisitive eyebrow. 'Yeah, you think so?'

'Sure, all saffron collectors are fairies – didn't you know that?'

'I guess I didn't.'

'It's just the same thing by another name.'

'Well, maybe you're right, sister…maybe you're right.'

Beatrice walked off with the watering can in her hands.

Teresa dug her own hands into the soil to reach down for the roots of the weeds. She needed to get to the roots. She had to plunge her hands deep into the earth.

The girls were all getting ready for bed. Alicia and Abigail were both gazing out of the window into the night sky. Summer evenings fell into darkness at a late hour. There was often a lightness to the night skies, as if the sun had extra-charged the planets to shine brighter. That night the girls were looking at another slither of light.

'I think its new moon tomorrow,' said Abigail, her face pressed close to the window. Resting against her shoulder was Alicia.

'Not long now,' added Tibia from where she was sitting on her bed. 'Are you ready?'

Alicia turned and brushed the hair from her face. 'I feel something different, inside – don't you?'

'Maybe you're growing your own saffron flower inside of you!' said Abigail as she gave Alicia a kiss on the cheek.

Teresa untied the white lace handkerchief from her hair. 'Maybe it's us who are going to be harvested.'

All the girls giggled – except Teresa. She wasn't sure if she was joking.

CHAPTER THIRTY - THREE

~ You are not here for your development – you are here for your unfolding ~

This time before the girls entered the study room there was a noticeable feeling of expectancy between them. Or rather, it was a quiet anxiousness. The new moon had arrived and with it La Madre's penultimate 'Spice Meeting,' as she had called their gatherings. The summer had been passing before them barely recognized. The summer days had moved swiftly between the intense hours of study, work responsibilities, and other forms of preparation. Only with the weekly games of *Saffron Softball* had the girls been able to engage in physical play. And even then it had been a form of 'disciplined play,' if there was such a term. Everything, it seemed, was directed toward some purpose and not the play of random events. All of the girls in the group of sixteen had felt this. Yet none more so than Teresa. If her body could be said to be vibrating, then it was literally buzzing.

The sixteen girls stepped into the room one by one at the invitation of La Madre's personal assistant, Madam Aisha. The upholstered chair with the delicate single-legged, circular wooden side table was arranged in the same manner as always. Upon the small side table stood the ceramic teapot with its decorated teacup. Inside the teapot, Teresa knew, was a hot brew of jasmine green tea.

La Madre came over from the far side of the room. She moved with grace and balance, as if each of her cells were in constant communication. She poured herself a cup of tea and then sat down with elegant ease. She lifted the tea cup to her nose and breathed in the vapour in what was a very careful and deliberate act. Then she took a sip of the tea before gently placing the cup back upon the table.

'You can sense the blend; the way it has come together. There is no mistaking the completeness, the wholeness of a thing.' La Madre slowly looked around the room at each of the girls. 'Today,' she continued, 'I wish to speak a little about the spice.'

Some of the girls twitched unconsciously as if the mere mention of the spice catalyzed a reaction in their bodies.

La Madre smiled, as if knowing. 'The saffron spice blends things together. It adds a special something to what already exists to create something else – something different from what was before. The spice is a catalyser. It knows how to take what was before and to re-blend. If there were no such blending functions in our world, it would have fallen apart by now. To blend is also to glue.'

La Madre brought the palms of her hands together and entwined them, her thin fingers overlapping her bony knuckles. Teresa noted that the skin on her hands was slightly wrinkled, although smooth.

'To blend is not to separate. If you take this, then you ignore *that*; and if you take only *that* then you ignore *this*. Only by blending them together can you produce a much finer force. We don't work with producing finished feasts or sumptuous treats – we work only with disseminating subtle flavours to assist in the process. And what is this process, you may ask? I tell you – it is the process of internally slow cooking the flavours required for human growth. The spice works with us, and in its sacrifice it does not reject anything that is worthy of its flavours.'

Something stirred within Teresa, as if a ball of energy had formed in the centre of her chest. That was it – that was the moment she *knew*.

La Madre shot Teresa a glance.

The older lady, looking refined and elegant in her chair, sipped carefully upon her teacup as if she had all the time in the world. Yet everyone in the room – especially La Madre – knew that, to the contrary, time was of the utmost essence. 'Almost everyone lacks an essential flavour in their life,' continued La Madre after putting down her teacup. 'No one is complete in this respect - or only the very few. Everyone else lacks. It is a simple fact, and very evident, and yet most people do not know this lack, or recognize it for what it is. They tell themselves it is something else – it is boredom, frustration, depression, career disappointment, or a broken heart. They call it many names. And yet they continue to fail to recognize it for what it is. Upon this earth, in *our* world, a special extra ingredient is always needed – no one can walk the way alone. Each person requires a touch of the spice, in one way or another. There are many ways the spice can be used – many, many subtle ways for it to enter into a person. Where there is lack, there is need. It is our function to recognize this need.'

Teresa recognized this last phrase immediately. It had been spoken only the other day by Madam Morag. It was as if the whole organism that was the Azafran Home for Girls was speaking with one voice – with one mind and one heart.

La Madre had paused yet again. Was it for the girls to

gather their thoughts, their attention – or had it been solely for Teresa to remember, record, and imprint within her that moment in time? And yet La Madre spoke to all of them, as if…as if they were one mind, one heart…one *golden thread…*

'To savour the nourishment and taste of the food, a person need not know – nor wish to know – the origin or specific use of each active ingredient. The function of the chef is to deliver the food in its best state for digestion and satisfaction – it doesn't come with the recipe attached. *You don't talk to people about recipes when you know they suffer from hunger.* To encourage young children to eat we often have to fly the food like an airplane into their mouths – we make it interesting, so the child wants to take it in. This is no different from how other nutrition is delivered to the people of this world!'

Some of the girls laughed. It was a peculiar image – of a spoonful of food flying into a baby's mouth. Yet when Teresa thought about it she knew it was also so, so right. La Madre smiled and nodded, as if she too was sharing, and savouring, the same image in her mind.

La Madre made a gentle cough, and silence returned to the room like a soft linen sheet laid across a bed.

'The power of the spice is that it is contagious. It contains a special ingredient - a unique centre of gravity - that can spread as a viral blessing. You could say that everything exists because of the spice, in whatever amount. It doesn't need to be in large quantities. It can be in the tiniest of drops, the thinnest of slithers. Yet it must be present. It is a part of our lives – for *all* of us – and vibrates through every living thing. Remember that all vibrations are contagious, whether for good or ill. We all exist in a contagious environment in which we must make our choices of which energy to share – the harmonious or the disharmonious. We are here to serve the transmission of the spice, and in this we are all contagious beings!' Saying this, La Madre let out one of her infrequent yet much loved laughs.

At the same time a beam of sunlight streamed through the glass window and fell across the room. It felt warm, as if a golden moment had come to participate in the shared love of the room. Like a puppy dog wagging its tail, the universe wished to show its affection. And for a brief moment the seconds stopped, the cosmos stopped spinning, nothing was real, everything was right – and everything just *was.*

Teresa's heart almost stopped too. At least it missed a beat or two. And then the world came back into being again. Teresa noticed that La Madre had been looking at her, and the feeling in that look melded something inside Teresa.

La Madre faced the class. 'Some people think that true

wisdom is a thing separate from life. Is the flavour of spice separate from the taste of the food? How can you expect to understand if you cannot place yourself *in* life and gain nourishment first from the world that surrounds you? Yes, it is a world of appearances; yet appearances appear to you for a reason. Learn from this first.'

La Madre created another one of her deliberate 'stop' moments by taking a long sip from her teacup. The moment – the words, the feeling – had been registered and imprinted. At least it had within Teresa.

'You are not here for your development – you are here for your unfolding. You already contain the essence; you cannot develop upon this, but you can allow it to unfold and spread out in the most correct and harmonious way. We don't deal with any add-ons here. We are not a factory with extra parts. Our concern is with what already exists in you – has always and will always exist. The question is – how can you bring it out into the world? Remember this - the spice brings out the best flavour with those who maintain their vital equilibrium.'

*Remember this…Remember this…*as the words entered within her Teresa felt as if a part of her – or the *her* itself - had just dislocated itself from the body.

'And then what will happen?'

Teresa looked over at Tibia who had just asked the question. They were both standing at one of the windows in the corridor that overlooked the large yard where they did gymnastics. The night sky was full of stars and resembled a roadmap of galaxies.

'I expect that after the first harvest they'll be another.'

'And then what?'

'And then another, and another,' replied Teresa as she gazed out.

'And how many more?' Tibia looked to be deep in thought.

'As many as it takes.'

'Why do you say that? It all sounds so vague.'

Teresa let out a low sigh. 'No, I think it's very clear. It will take as many as it takes until *we get it*. The harvest is about us. The saffron flowers get put in the ground every spring, and their spice is harvested in the autumn. But we are always in the soil, in the earth, and we are always growing…and we can be harvested anytime, once we are ready. And then, and only then, can we carry the spice with us.'

Tibia turned to look at Teresa. 'Why do you say that? How do you know?'

'I don't know. I just…sense…'

A star shot across the sky and fizzled out.

CHAPTER THIRTY - FOUR

*~ Humanity, in its natural state, seeks to be in
harmony with its world ~*

All the girls mingled on the grassy field. The last game of *Saffron Softball* had been arranged to mark the end of the summer season, and to mark the imminent arrival of the harvest.

Teresa stood at one side of the field, alone, considering what she was going to say to her team. At that moment the figure of La Madre appeared, almost suddenly by her side. 'You didn't think I would miss the final game of the season, did you?'

Teresa smiled. 'I somewhat hoped you wouldn't.'

La Madre was holding a parasol to keep shaded from the morning sun.

'No, I could hardly keep away. After all, it's such a wondrous game. How did you come up with it?'

Teresa shrugged. 'I don't know. It just kind of came to me one day.'

'How interesting!'

Teresa sensed a deliberate false naivety on the part of La Madre. She turned to look into the face of the older lady. La Madre's eyes twinkled, almost mischievously.

'Yes, quite a coincidence,' replied Teresa in a similar tone. 'Isn't it!'

'Like I was just compelled to come up with the idea.'

'Indeed.'

'As if it was somehow a good idea to bring all the girls together. It's almost as if the sport was not the reason at all – but just *being together*.'

'Mm…interesting, isn't it?' This time it was La Madre who turned toward Teresa. 'Just being together; I like that thought.'

'Indeed,' replied Teresa. 'It's as if our being together makes a connection with something else…somewhere else.'

'Now, whatever gave you that idea, my dear?' La Madre smiled and walked away to join some of the other Madams on the field.

Indeed, whispered Teresa under her breath.

Teresa had told her team to think of the game as a whole body. Every part must work together, organically, in harmony. Also that everyone must adapt to the game, and not be rigid. No pattern ever repeats itself, she had told her team mates. Playing the game was not about expecting things to happen, it was about *feeling into* each moment.

'I want you to feel each of the other players,' she had said. 'They are not your opponents – they are other parts of yourself.' Each of the other girls in her team listened to Teresa. They respected her, and had already noticed the insights that Teresa often had.

'Don't play for yourself, and don't play for me either,' Teresa had said. 'Play for that which is bigger than all of us. Play for that part of yourself that knows there is a reason for this that is both all of us together and yet so much more. Play for all those *togethers* that unite into one. Play for your sisters, for the human race, for all the earth…play for the stars, the heavens, and everything that ever existed. If you don't play for the evermore – for the *all that is* – then you are just playing your own little game. And then it's your own little world. And all your meanings will stop once the game finishes. Let's take away something bigger – *something beyond.* Let's be a part of that special ingredient which is in every atom and every heart. Let's play with reverence – with love!'

Teresa had let the words fall from her lips. When she had finished all the girls were looking at her with wonder in their faces…and almost tears in their eyes. It was as if they had just realized, in that very moment, that life was…was so much more – and in that understanding there was so much beauty the human body could hardly contain it.

The team silently came together and shared a hug.

Yes…thought Teresa – it was all about being together.

Madam Morag was re-stacking the books upon their shelves when Teresa entered the library. The younger girl stood silently, observing the older lady as she picked up a book and ran her hand along the shelves before placing it in a slot.
'You seem to know where all the books fit in.'
Madam Morag smiled but neither turned her head nor answered.
Teresa observed for a few minutes more before she realized something. 'You're not even reading the classification numbers!'
Madam Morag simply shrugged. 'The books know where they go.'
Teresa walked up until she was beside Madam Morag. 'How

do you know that?' she asked after observing a while longer. 'The books have their correct places. Everything has an essential harmony. It's when we disrupt that harmony that we get problems. And believe me, it is us who do the disrupting. So, let it all come together.'

After several more minutes Madam Morag finished what she was doing and went over to another table where a pile of books stood. She motioned for Teresa to follow her.

'Here, why don't you try it? Go on, place the books where you know they should go – and don't read the spines!'

Teresa picked up one of the books and turned it around in her hands. She felt the book, but not between her fingers.

The older lady observed her. 'Just like you did in the game this morning – trust in that harmony. Whether softball or book, you know how it works.'

And saying that, Madam Morag walked away, leaving Teresa alone.

CHAPTER THIRTY - FIVE

~ Your role is to provide for others, for those that do not know or suspect ~

The night before had seen the moon full. It had hung in the sky like a giant circular ship, observing over the Azafran Home for Girls.

That morning all the girls on the corridor awoke early with anticipation in their bones. Today was to be the final Spice Meeting with La Madre. Excitedly they all washed themselves amid a buzz of whisperings and giggles and the odd nudging. The last of the spice meetings also signalled that harvesting was near, and this was the real reason that energized the sixteen girls as they got ready for the day ahead.

Autumn had arrived and yet the warm days continued. In their part of the world where the Azafran Home stood, the days were long, the light was bright, and the winters were shorter. And it was an ideal seasonal climate for the saffron flowers to grow in the fields; an ideal climate also for the girls to be nurtured along the saffron way.

The study room, adjacent to the library, was buzzing with vibrant feminine energy. The room felt like a hot bed for the nurturing of seeds into flowers; and from flowers into the flow of their essences. Whether nectar or spice, the essence of each living thing seeks release and communion within the same moment.

The steam from the teapot was visible as it nuzzled against the stray beams of autumnal sunlight entering the room. La Madre was already seated in her chair before the girls entered slowly. There was serenity to the older woman's face as she gazed across the room and at the faces of the younger girls. Teresa could not be sure whether such calmness was because of this particular moment or because La Madre had presided over this moment on numerous occasions and all the memories were now converging within her into one.

'Our final full moon has arrived and the path of the saffron collector stands before us.' As La Madre spoke a silence came over the room that seemed to connect all senses into one shared collective. All eyes, ears, and hearts were focused upon the seated lady who now, Teresa noted, suddenly appeared delicate for the first time. Her frame was thin and almost fragile, shielded behind the folds of her long, flowing white dress. All hearts in the room beat within their expectant hosts' bodies until it seemed they entrained and beat as one.

La Madre leant forward slightly, as if to project the meaning of her words further into the room. 'Let us speak today about the saffron collector, for the harvest is soon upon us. The saffron collector is a fugitive in this world – an inside outsider who holds the cup full of deepest and sweetest appreciation and gratitude. The saffron collector observes two fundamental states of being simultaneously – freedom and servitude. These two states are not contradictory, as they may appear to be, but when in proper relation are in fact extremely complementary. As you will come to learn and understand, true freedom is to be in service. And true service brings with it an ultimate freedom. It is only the opinions and false perceptions of this world that create the contradictions and confusion. The path of the saffron collector is incredibly harmonious – as it needs to be. The manner in which the saffron flower provides its spice is a harmonious act. There is no contradiction or conflict in the giving of this precious gift. So too should we reflect this natural harmony in our own lives. If in our daily lives there exists an uncomfortable friction, or a conflict of energies, then we are not doing something right. This discomfort is a sign of some misalignment – a sign that something about our behaviour, our manner, our state, is not in harmony with the natural forces of life. Humanity, in its natural state, seeks to be in harmony with its world. The disharmony that exists in the world outside of here is an external reflection of humanity's collective internal disarray. The sharing of the saffron spice is one way that seeks to lessen this disarray and to seek the natural way of harmony.'

La Madre paused to take a sip of her tea. No one in the room moved. Everyone was still, silent, without a breeze to sway their petals. Inside each of them the spice was unfurling and coming closer to maturation.

'You will not be empty by giving,' continued La Madre. 'On the contrary, you will be filled, restored, so that you have more to give. Do not be that person who unknowingly takes away from others – your role is to provide for others, for those that do not know or suspect.'

A broad smile broke out upon the older lady's face as if some humorous spice had just trickled down her throat and melted into the tissues and fibre of her body. 'The saffron flowers laugh with us, becoming our mouths and voice, in praise of the sun. Saffron flowers have their own unique, fragrant language – they speak so softly we have to strain our senses to hear. The saffron fragrance praises each new day – they are the secret companions to the world.'

La Madre looked around the room and gazed into the eyes of each young girl. She looked past their iris gateways and into the deeper seat where each essence lay nestled. 'We are here to blossom like the saffron flowers – in adoration of the invisible spirit that blows through us. The saffron flowers are also messengers. They can transmit your messages, or the messages of others, if you know this art of communication. I have received many messages from my saffron flowers. A person must be very receptive and extremely attentive to receive and understand such messages. That is why, originally, we placed flowers on the grave of a loved one – the flowers were entrusted with a message that we sent to our loved ones on the other side.'

At that moment the door to the study room opened and Madam Aisha walked in with a small plant pot. She carefully placed the pot on the table beside the teapot and, as if everything was choreographed, walked out again without a word or a nod. La Madre bent over to cup the lilac petals of the flower in her hands. She closed her eyes as she smelled the flower. When she opened her eyes again Teresa thought she saw a twinkle in the older woman's eyes as if reflecting a star from the heavens above.

'I had this one planted slightly earlier,' said La Madre, and allowed herself a private chuckle. 'It's an old custom of mine, to receive the first saffron flower of the season. I'm sure you can all forgive an older lady her little whims!'

A great wave of love rippled across the room that embraced everybody. Teresa felt it engulf her and squeeze her body tightly as if it was a warm overcoat protecting her.

'The golden thread,' whispered La Madre. She then reached out and gently touched the petals of the saffron flower. 'Yes, yes,' she said softly under her breath as if talking only to herself.

La Madre turned to face the rest of the young faces in the room. 'Let us say that there is a certain knowing which comes from the spice of the saffron flower. This knowing should not be shared until you have experienced the taste of the spice for yourself. This is necessary to help in the maturation of the spice. Most people, rightly so, do not concern themselves with this. The way of the saffron operates well beyond them. As such, most of the people of this world have no concept of what we do. You may well be asking yourself what it is that we *really* do. The answer is that we give without anyone knowing that we give. And do you wish to know what the hardest part of what we do is? It is to behave as a normal person.'

Again, La Madre leant forward slightly in her chair. 'For those of us who work with the spice of the saffron there are four hands we work with: patience, compassion, understanding…and doing the little things.' She then sat back and closed her eyes.

La Madre remained with her eyes closed for several minutes, and yet the time seemed not to know how to pass. Teresa felt timelessness in that moment, as if the room was situated in the centre of everything – in the heart of the cosmos; an axial upon which the heavens turned.

Teresa also knew – she *felt* – that La Madre was creating a moment, a protected space, where the significance of what she had just said could be absorbed. La Madre needed a little time before she could continue with the next stage of the harvest. Every thing in nature requires its time of nurture.

'There,' said La Madre, 'let us continue.'

'Let us continue along the path before us – the path we have all walked since first entering this place. This path – this *way* – is known as the way of the saffron. The way of the saffron is not about seeking the sublime, or feeling blessed, or being radiant – and all the rest of these fanciful terms. It is about hard work, proper alignment, and providing a service to the visible and invisible worlds according to the greater need. And no one may thank you for it – except the light within each atom that will shine because of what you do. Yet rest assured, we do not work alone – no one works alone upon the saffron path. The work we do does not come from one person alone, and nor is it for one person to receive alone. There are others who do similar work to ours, and yet they are not like us, nor we like them. And there is a very good reason for that. For what we do requires a very specific preparation. Everything that has occurred here in this place – under the auspices of the Azafran Foundation - has been to prepare you so that you may be ready to receive this path. For in order to give – to transmit – we must first have the capacity to receive, otherwise no transmission is possible. Our bodies as well as our spirit are required for this purpose. If this was not the case then biological life on this planet would be directed toward another function – a different *potential*. But no – the human biological apparatus has its function as do other forms in Nature. The human body is like a mould that we pour the spice into.'

As La Madre said this she picked up her teapot and slowly poured the tea into her cup until it was full.

'As a mould the body has its limitations; yet as a vessel it has great potential to adapt to the treasures it can receive. Trust that your body, whilst physically rigid, is indeed a wonderfully versatile companion and host. And as a host it serves as a conduit – as a thoroughfare, you may say. The spice functions and works through people, and has always done so. It is not an abstract thing - an ethereal, vague notion. It is not an Expressionist painting or a surreal poem. It is something incredibly real; and if used in the right way has immense power to operate through, and with, people across this planet. The saffron flower knows this, and allows herself to be cultivated for this use. It is a tradition as old as the seeds of the flower…as old as the seeds of humanity. And certain aware individuals have acted as the seeds for human society, just like the cells in the human body. They act upon the culture they are in for the benefit of the larger body. These impulses largely go unrecognized, and yet they are crucial for the life of the body. Cultures, like the saffron flowers, require the necessary ingredients of right nutrition, right timing – the planting and harvesting - and fertile soil. We do not plant the saffron bulbs in winter. Nor do we plant them in arid soil. Human cultures require the same considerations. A culture must have various generative seeds that are allowed to germinate in prepared soil, under the correct conditions. As you may have realized, this is a feminine process. The seeding, germinating, and nurturing within a body are all aspects of the feminine. There are other *active* elements that must be combined to this, yet this is not our domain. We work with our qualities, with the essential nature of the spice. The saffron collector has her essential work to deliver, which although may go unnoticed is of the greatest service. We operate within the body of the world, in cultures we can move around in easily, and we are known only by our exterior faces. Yet *we* recognize each other. There is nothing nobler than the inward recognition of two souls. Now we embark upon our way, in the manner most suited to each of us; in service most appropriate to our capacity. And this is indeed a most wondrous blessing and privilege. It is an honour to play our part, not only for the human species but also for our grand cosmic family. This is our function – and this is our harvesting.'

At this point La Madre stood up and walked toward the sixteen girls who were all seated on the floor before her. Instinctively all the girls stood up at once and allowed La Madre to walk into their midst, like entering a sacred circle. The girls gathered around her, enclosing the elder lady within their centre. Again, as if in silent communion, all sixteen girls held hands as they circled the figure of La Madre. They moved slowly in an anti-clockwise direction whilst the central figure turned slowly in a contrary clockwise direction. The outer and inner circles moved like this, slowly at first, gaining momentum. Then the circles turned faster and faster…

…Teresa felt as if her body had entered a trance. Her legs were moving, her eyes were closed…the circle turned faster…faster…moving, moving as one…the circle kept moving…there was no time…no sense…no outward orientation…minutes…more…longer…contraction… expansion…a tingling…a rise…an energy…then… *something shifted…*

Teresa's eyes remained closed as she lay upon her bed. It was late, at the end of the day, and yet sleep was far away. Teresa was trying to process what had happened earlier in the day. She had sensed communion with the saffron flower – with the spice. And importantly, she had sensed the presence of the golden thread. But not only had she sensed it but she had also seen it with her inner eye. It had connected all of them, and had tied the two circles together. She had seen it weave around each girl as it then connected with La Madre in the centre. She had *seen* La Madre in her mind's eye, with her arms open and whirling in the centre of the circle – two arms stretched open with the golden thread connecting to her feminine centre. And Teresa had felt it too...*everything*. And there had been movement within her...a very pleasurable feeling - an explosion within the body that sparkled like an effervescence of stardust...there were no more words for it. Only the words of La Madre echoing within her - *Let us remember, deep in our hearts, and deeper in our self, that if the outer sun rises but the inner sun does not, then nothing has been gained.*

CHAPTER THIRTY - SIX

~ Where there is no harmony – no grace – there is no true correspondence ~

The days after at the Azafran Home for Girls were different. They were now ready for the harvesting. After the previous full moon they had to wait a little longer until the fourth quarter of the moon's cycle had arrived. When the moon's gravitational pull is weaker, La Madre had said, it is her resting period. It is then that the saffron flowers will be ready for harvesting. It is then that the spice will be most receptive.

Crocus sativus - the saffron crocus - a lilac-coloured flower containing at its centre the three-branched stigma of feminine spice. The three burnt-sun golden stigmas waiting for the prepared hand to pluck them out. Receptive, waiting, giving – like three cords of a golden lyre they wait for the right tune to release them…

…the girls awoke before dawn as the moist air lay across the land of mother Earth. This was to be their first day of harvesting, and each heart, each hand, each knot upon the golden thread was ready…was prepared…

HARVEST

The Saffron Collector is a fugitive in this world – an inside outsider who holds the cup full of deepest and sweetest appreciation and gratitude.

CHAPTER THIRTY - SEVEN

*~ The spice reflects back the transcendence that lies at
the heart of the cosmos ~*

Snatching saffron flowers in the morning before the sun rising. Plucking the crimson stigmata carefully by hand and then drying the saffron threads under the sun to create the spice. Working with the four hands of the saffron collector - patience, compassion, understanding…and those little things. Great work for small quantities. Yet there is no qualifying the value of the spice when it comes from the hands of the true saffron collector.

These were the days of the harvest, and Teresa along with the other girls had participated in the harvest of each following year. And now, after several years of harvests, they were once again drying the saffron in the sun to make the spice. The sixteen girls had learnt the art of transformation – transforming the saffron bulbs into flowers and then into dried spice. Theirs was now a world where transformation was contagious.

Teresa was now twenty-three years old, as were Tibia and Beatrice. Alicia and Abigail were each twenty-five whilst the youngest amongst them, Simone, was twenty-two. These six girls had become a close group over the intervening years. And those years had been even more intense than the ones leading up to their first harvest. Whenever one reached a plateau, it seemed, greater effort was required to push past it. Otherwise, as La Madre had said, one remains marooned upon their own island, content to think that the end had been reached when one is still adrift. The only way for the saffron collector was forward – always moving forward and never treading water.

The way forward was through each yearly planting and harvesting of the saffron flowers. And those harvest mornings before sunrise were special days. Not only were they days of alignment, communion, and connection. They were also days of careful attention to the tiniest of details.

Before the sun rises the saffron crocus flowers are closed in slumber. They awaken their petals to the sun's warm hands and their stigmata absorb the radiant energy.

The saffron collectors must work fast to pick as many saffron crocuses as possible before the sun's presence intervenes and snatches her children back from the hands of the human collectors.

The sixteen girls are all seated around the large wooden table in silence. They work in communion, connected by the golden thread within. Their nimble fingers snatch the three fiery stigmas from the centre, from the heart of the saffron crocus. The sun-burnt saffron stigmata are then laid on a large white cloth and offered to the sun as she rises high in the sky. They are burnt again for yet another time. This time the stigmas are without their mother crocus. And this time the heat of the furnace burns so hot that the final transformation is accomplished. The stigmas are no more. Now they have become their full potential – they have become the spice.

The spice reflects back the transcendence that lies at the heart of the cosmos.

Teresa was seated at the far end of the large yard, on a bench under shade. At the other far end she could see the water well, with its opening still covered with gauze. It had been many years now since she had first peered into its darkened opening. Since then no little girls had fallen down into its watery throat. That was the day Teresa had received her white laced handkerchief from La Madre. The same white handkerchief which still adorned her hair. The years had been many, and yet so few. It was difficult to know how exactly the years had moulded her from the inside out. There were some things at the Azafran Home for Girls that were indeed contagious.

Teresa stepped back within herself and observed the activity going on around her. Some of the girls would be leaving soon, she knew. And new young faces would be entering too. There would be another gymnastics instructor to teach the young ones, just as Anna had done with them. The Work would continue – for La Madre and for all of them.

La Madre was getting older and frailer.

CHAPTER THIRTY - EIGHT

*~ We each have a golden thread within us that is the
timelessness out of which the cosmos is ceaselessly born ~*

She saw the expression on Madam Aisha's face as she entered the room. These days fewer people entered La Madre's private quarters. The demands of time upon the matriarch of the home had only increased and not lessened with the years. Just as she had done so eighteen years before, as a five-year-old girl, Teresa stepped lightly into the room where sunrays were casting their glance. La Madre was standing at the far end beside her bookshelves, her hands folded in front of her, gazing across the many book titles and names. Teresa quietly walked over.

La Madre turned around to face her and smiled.

'Faces are better than names – and much easier to remember too!' The elder lady's face shone with an inner warmth and compassion. Teresa noticed the deep wrinkles that now framed her features, lines that marked an unknown terrain. 'La Madre, you're still doing too much.' There was an imploring tone in Teresa's voice. Yet she knew her plea would fall upon a deliberate deafness. Inside of her, Teresa knew that a great deal was still needed to be done and that La Madre was needed now as much as ever.

'Yes, my dear. But it is a *doing* that calls to me from out of timelessness. And this is what connects us all so that my work is made possible, made lighter, by all of you doing your work. It's similar to your game of *Saffron Softball* – when you arrive at the playing field you expect your team mates to be there, ready and prepared for the game. You also expect that the arbitrators are there to observe and score points; and you expect, and require, the tools – the bat and the ball. Now if you arrived at the playing field and these things were not in their place…well, you would not be able to have your game. It is the same here at the Azafran Home for Girls. If people do not do their preparation – *their work* – then I cannot do mine. Really, I am here because of you.' La Madre waggled a finger at Teresa and grinned. 'Of course, we each have a golden thread within us that is the timelessness out of which the cosmos is ceaselessly born. Growing old, dear child, is only the flakes that fall from an outer skin. We always were, and always shall be.' La Madre's eyes twinkled and radiated an empathy that bathed Teresa. At this moment she felt so much love for the older lady – her friend, her mentor, her mother.

La Madre casually cast her hand over the bookshelves. 'These have their purpose, and shall be useful too for the next one. Some of them, though, will not be used.' La Madre gave Teresa a sharp, penetrating look. 'Each text is an instrument, a tool, which must function correct to its time. The work of the saffron collector must be renewed for each new era, for circumstances and contexts always change. But you already know that, Teresa.'

La Madre moved away from the shelves and went to sit down in her large comfortable chair. 'You're probably wondering why I called for you here?'

Teresa walked over to where La Madre sat and placed her hand gently upon her shoulder.

'There doesn't have to be a reason, mother. I would be here anytime for you.'

'You are a good one, my child. You are as pure as saffron petals and as burnt inside as the spice.'

Teresa smiled. She had indeed over the eighteen years been burnt inside by the heatless fire.

La Madre's face suddenly went expressionless and cold. 'I have to tell you that I am waiting. I am waiting before I can go. And until that waiting ceases, I cannot see you again. Do not come to see me again until I wait no more.' La Madre turned her head away.

Teresa had been dismissed. Her stomach clenched tight as if holding inside a bodily prisoner.

She closed the door behind her as she stepped out of La Madre's private quarters. It was true, so true, and Teresa knew it – had always known it. Now she had to find it again – that one thing that she knew mattered the most.

CHAPTER THIRTY - NINE

*~ Each human being is like the seed of a flower, awaiting
to pollinate in the world ~*

The day had an ominous feel to it, as if some underlying cords were being plucked. The girls didn't have to say anything – they just *knew*. They felt the golden thread being strung out into new patterns, new directions. There was a hidden hand coming into the centre of their tightly-knit pattern and rearranging it.

The girls cast uneasy glances in the bathroom and yet no one spoke. Teresa could herself feel the pounding – even hear it – as if all hearts beating were being heard. It was a feeling, a sensation that Teresa knew she would have to get accustomed to over the years. She didn't know how she knew this…she just knew it. And she also knew that it was a sensation that La Madre had always had to live with, and was still living with.

Despite being dismissed from La Madre's presence, and told not to visit her again, Teresa was feeling *closer* to her mentor rather than further away. After a day's sullenness and deep introspection Teresa had finally realized what it was that La Madre was waiting for – what she really wanted. No, not wanted – what she needed. The dismissal had been a call, a reminder that if there ever was a time then it had to be now. Teresa told herself that she would make the visit to La Madre later in the evening. First she had to get through the day. And she had the gut feeling that it was going to be a day she would always remember above many others.

Teresa went to the library to look for Madam Morag. She had a wish to speak with her. Somehow Teresa thought that it might help; that the older Madam would be able to provide some framing for her own thoughts. Yet Madam Morag was nowhere to be found. The library was open, yet her office was locked and her usual presence was absent.

Teresa decided to go to the kitchens to see if she could speak with Madam Pym, who was usually a lively force. When she arrived she found that the dining hall was busy with activity. Many of the younger girls were hurriedly cleaning and tidying the hall whilst a few of the older girls, such as Beatrice and Simone, were helping Madam Pym to move some of the tables aside. Madam Pym looked up as Teresa entered the hall but quickly carried on with her work. It was obvious to Teresa that the large Madam was in no mood, or position, to entertain her questions. As Teresa was leaving the hall she almost ran into Madam Celia who was coming in. Teresa offered her apologies and as she spoke she realized there was something slightly different about Madam Celia. She still had the thin, slender face that perched on top of her tall, slim frame. That was it – Madam Celia had newly dyed her hair. It was much more reddish than usual, and almost shimmering against the natural skin of her face. Newly dyed hair – what was so special about the day?

Behind Madam Celia came the wide-eyed innocent faces.

The group of them entered the hall all holding hands in a chain. *The Golden thread*, thought Teresa, as she watched the new arrivals weave into the room. They all looked so young! They could be no more than...

'Five years old. One of them is six and another is four. The rest are five years old.'
Teresa looked up into Madam Celia's eyes.
'Yes,' continued the Madam, 'exactly the same age as when

you arrived. Or perhaps you no longer remember that? I dyed my hair for that day too.' Madam Celia smiled and gave Teresa a knowing look. 'But you're not the young girl any more, are you? You've become quite the madam yourself!' Madam Celia carried on with the chain of young girls in tow. 'Come on girls – lots of new things to show you!'

Teresa watched as the trail of young bodies entered into the heart of the Azafran Home.

If something new enters then something old must leave. There always had to be a harmony, a balance. It was like circulation in the body, as La Madre had often spoken of. She had likened the saffron collectors to the blood of the body, to the life flow. As there is breath in, there is breath out – the inhale, the exhale. There would be some saffron collectors leaving that same day. All the girls had known it and yet none could speak of it.

Teresa's instinct sent her back to her dormitory room. She stepped inside with an expectant heart. All the beds were made, exactly as they had left them. Only that the room looked more bare than usual. Gone were many of the personal items. Teresa should have known.

La Madre had prepared them for this. She had told them, in her kind voice and loving eyes, that each and every human being is like the seed of a flower, awaiting to pollinate in the world. The spice was being disseminated – the harvest spreading further afield.

Teresa was walking back down the large stone staircase as she crossed with Madam Morag. Neither of them said a word. They didn't need to – a look was enough.

They were waiting. All of them were waiting. Everyone knew. Even Teresa herself knew. So why had she held it off for so long? She recalled the words of La Madre as they fell as charms into her ears – *true freedom is having no choice.*

Madam Aisha opened the door to let her in.

CHAPTER FORTY

*~ Sacrifice is everything and nothing - it is the radiant
heart and the receptive womb~*

La Madre sat by the shuttered window in her favourite chair. Teresa, feeling like a little girl, stepped quietly into the room, not wishing to make a sound. Not wishing to disturb the speckles of dust drifting through the almost still air. It felt like her first day all over again. Only this time La Madre looked frailer; an older flower catching the warmth of the sun. La Madre knew that Teresa had come, yet she did not move. It was as if she wanted to deliberately show this personal, fragile side of her. As if a deliberate dropping of her guard to let another see inside, beyond the boundary, if only for the briefest of moments. Both women remained in silence; one the observer, the other the observed. And in that thread of time both ladies were sharing a private embrace. It was also a silent acknowledgement – a special privilege.

Finally, La Madre turned her head and gave Teresa a smile.

'Come here, my dear.'

Teresa quietly walked over. When she came to where La Madre was sitting she bent over a placed a slight kiss upon her forehead. La Madre reached up and took her hand.

'Sorry it has taken me so long,' said Teresa in a soft voice.

'Do not worry, my child. It took as long as it needed to. For you that is. The truth of it was never in doubt. It was known all along.'

La Madre motioned for Teresa to sit on a stool in front of her.

'Is my waiting over?' La Madre gave Teresa a questioning look, yet in her eyes there was a river of warmth.

Teresa nodded. She leant forward so that her face was closer to the older lady. Then she said softly – 'it is sacrifice. The essence of the saffron spice is that it sacrifices everything. It gives all of its flavour, its properties, its aspects – gives all of itself to those who receive. And in return for this sacrifice it receives everything – it is complete.'

La Madre closed her eyes and breathed deeply several times. When she opened her eyes again there was a deep, faraway look in them.

Teresa had understood the essence of the saffron. The realization had come to her from the penultimate spice meeting when La Madre had talked about the spice and a ball of energy had formed in Teresa's chest. And it was for this understanding that La Madre had been waiting to receive.

La Madre reached out and took both of Teresa's hands in her own. Teresa then understood herself that La Madre had known all along. As if recognizing this thought the older ladý nodded and gave a wink.

'Some things just *are,* Teresa. The rest is waiting – waiting until the already known becomes conscious. I have been waiting many days for your arrival, yet I never once doubted this moment would come. There are no doubts when dealing with the essence of the spice. Everything has its need, and such needs have their time. Everything else is often imagination, distraction, or human hesitation. But for the flowers – and for all the beautiful life in Nature – there is a different time. Theirs is the time of the natural flow. It is a flow of harmony and necessity. It is a grand pattern where all the threads are woven. In this there lies also the golden thread, with its own grander pattern. It is both within Nature, and humanity, and also with the greater Light. The way of the saffron must continue to weave this golden thread through all of life. And now the way requires another heart, a young heart, for mine is growing tired. What is being asked is a great sacrifice. The way of the saffron has always demanded this sacrifice, and all those called have made the gift. Sacrifice is everything and nothing - it is the radiant heart and the receptive womb. It is how the cosmos loves, and to sacrifice is the greatest love.

La Madre reached up her hands towards Teresa's head and gently pulled her forward. She then slipped her hands to the back and untied the white laced handkerchief from her hair. She placed the handkerchief in Teresa's hands and then squeezed them tight. 'This is for the next one, my dear.'

The both of them sat in silence, hands entwined, breathing gently together as one.

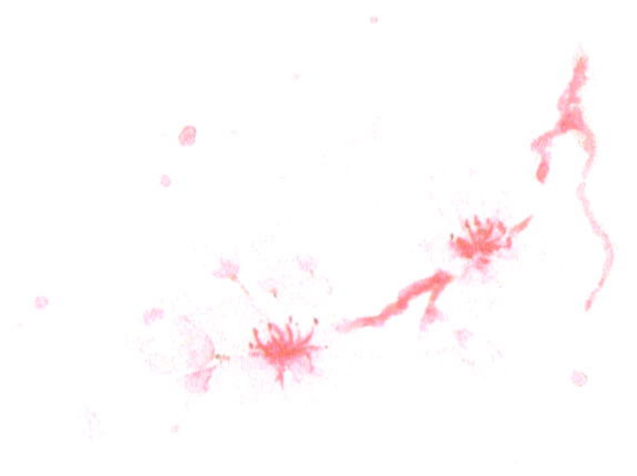

CHAPTER FORTY - ONE

~ The human heart reflects the purposeful patterns of the
cosmos ~

Tibia was on the rooftop terrace gazing up into the night sky, her head pulled back. She didn't say anything as Teresa approached. It had been a long day. There had been many changes at the Azafran Home for Girls. The two girls stood side by side and craned their necks upwards to receive the starlight from far, far away.

'I'm glad you're still here, Tibia.'

The short-haired girl turned and looked at her friend with the long, dark hair.

'I'm glad I'm here too, with you.' Then she noticed something had changed. 'Your hair isn't tied back – where is your white handkerchief?'

'It's gone now.' Teresa looked into Tibia's face and recognized the friend she needed.

'Like Abigail and Alicia – they're gone too!' Tibia's eyes showed moisture.

Teresa nodded. 'Some of us need to disperse into the world – that is our way.'

'I'm still here – and so are you!'

'I'm going to need you, Tibia. Will you help me?'

'Of course!' Tibia gave her friend a hug. Teresa embraced her friend back, although she felt a slight reticence in her body. 'You know I'd always help you.'

'Yeah, I guess I always did know that,' replied Teresa with a smile.

'And what else?'

'What else?' Teresa looked at her friend, and knew what she meant. 'Some things are going to change, and some things will remain the same. That's the way it's always been.'

'Are any more girls leaving us?'

Teresa nodded. 'Some more will need to leave. There is a necessity for them in the world. At the same time we have our new intake.'

'New young souls stepping onto the path of the saffron collector.' Tibia gazed once more into the starry night with a smile on her face. Then she let out a sigh. 'Remember all those years ago, Teresa? Remember us? The tree in the field, the rain, the well…all those years ago now.'

'Yes – all those years ago. And as we get older time moves faster.'

'Why is that?'

'Our bodies, our cells, they all vibrate faster – it's the quickening. As we get closer to maturity, the quickening happens. Just like the spurt in Nature before the blossoming.'

'And after maturity, is there still the quickening?'

'Yes – the quickening towards decay and renewal.'

'And the future – *our* future?'

'Our future is here, Tibia. If you accept to stay here with me then we will stay here until we are old…old like the Madams already here.'

'And then?'

'And then we too shall finally leave the nest and enter the world – but it will be a different world. If you accept, Tibia.' Tibia looped her arm round Teresa's. 'Yes, I accept. I'm staying here for as long as you are here. I'm not going anywhere. The way of the saffron for me is here – this is my path. And La Madre?

This time it was Teresa who sighed. 'The La Madre that we know and love shall soon be leaving us.'

Tibia's face grew sad. Teresa drew Tibia close to her as if to reassure her. 'But the essence of the spice remains…it has been passed on.'

Tibia didn't say anything. She listened to her breath rise and fall beneath a canopy of stars.

By the time the first light of dawn arrived things at the Azafran Home for Girls had already changed. Tibia awoke sensing a different atmosphere as if there was a new scent in the air. The first thing she did was to look across to Teresa's bed.

It was empty. Her best friend was gone.

MARIA

Be tireless, be loving - be the true feminine of this earth. There is nothing greater, more beautiful, or more fulfilling

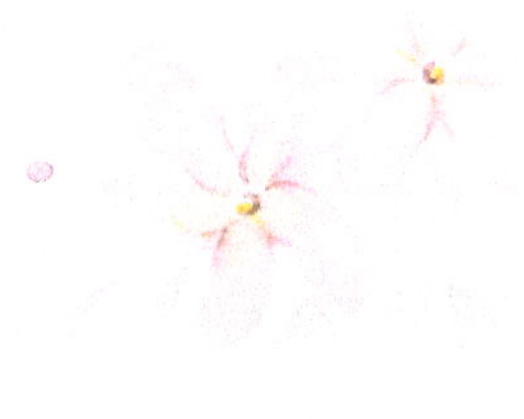

CHAPTER FORTY - TWO

~ The Earth is one mother among many ~

The little girl stepped quietly into the room, not wishing to make a sound. Not wishing to disturb the speckles of dust drifting through the rays of the sun. The morning light had risen early, as it did during the summer days. The heat was also beginning to rise up, getting ready to infiltrate through the slightly parted window. The tiniest of breezes brought in a whisper of scent as the last traces of jasmine, the lady of the night, crept in. The little girl stood still, waiting patiently. Her senses were alert, watching for signs, eager to pick up on any clues. She could hear the sound of her heart as it pumped inside of her chest. She was young, and yet she had learnt how to be observant. She also knew, in some way, that her being here meant something.

Her eyes lighted upon the figure seated near the window.

Maria was four years old. Entering the room of La Madre was one of her earliest, most definable memories. It was in that moment – in that soft-scented room where shade and light mingled together – that everything began. All previous happenings were now divorced from her life the instant Maria had stepped into the room. She would always recollect that sun-sprinkled morning as the first day of her life. That was the first time she had ever met La Madre, and first meetings never come again no matter how hard you wish for them. They are precious, like a golden moment.

CHAPTER FORTY - THREE

~ For you are the sun, the moon, the rain, and the heartbeat ~

It had been many, many years since Teresa whispered the secret of the saffron's essence into the ears of La Madre. And in those intervening years La Madre had not only revealed the greater confluence of essences but had also fulfilled her promise regarding the revelation of the spice. The revelation had taken many years, for its preparation and transmission. And now Teresa was its custodian. There had always been spice in the world - and as long as there were those prepared to maintain the transmission, so it would always continue to be.

Teresa remembered clearly in her mind the final

words of La Madre.

'I've had my girls around me, now you shall have yours. You are not alone – the spice does not permit this. You will be assisted in everything you do. Trust your friends – your Madams – for they are more than your family now. They have become parts of your body. You exist as an organic unit, sharing thoughts, knowing and understanding together. The Madre is just the extended heart - the Madams shall be your organs, the Azafran Home shall be your body, and the saffron collectors shall be like your blood. As the earth is a body, so are we. As is the macro, so is the micro. And the spice is the *special ingredient* that humanity needs to continue growing upon this most beautiful planet. It is such a great blessing that is bestowed upon you; and yet the most demanding of work. Be tireless, be loving - be the true feminine of this earth. There is nothing greater, more beautiful, or more fulfilling. It is the All, and none can know of it who does not partake. Great love, blessed daughter of the earth, for you are the sun, the moon, the rain, and the heartbeat. You are everything and you are nothing. You are of the soil and of the spirit. Embrace all, and be embraced by all. Leave nothing untouched…great, great love. Go now, and take care of the saffron flowers for me.'

La Madre had left, taking all her Madams with her, except one. The Azafran Home for Girls continued along its known path; the large building being a school, a body, and an ark.

CHAPTER FORTY - FOUR

*~ As it has always been, so it shall
always continue to be ~*

Maria quietly left the room, her mind and body filled with new sensations. Outside of the private quarters La Madre's personal secretary, Madam Tibia, was waiting for her. The older lady took the young girl's hand and walked with her into the corridor.

'This is your new home now, Maria. You will learn lots of new things here and make many new friends. I am sure you are going to like it here. The Azafran Home takes good care of its girls.'

'La Madre?' asked the little girl in a whisper.

Madam Tibia smiled and softly stroked the young girl's hair.

'Yes, La Madre too. She takes very good care of all her children here. Yes, especially La Madre.'

Madam Tibia took the young girl down to the communal dining hall to meet the others. When they arrived Maria saw that there were other young girls there like her. They all had the same expressions on their faces, as if they had been caught in a beam of starlight. Maria recognized this as the expression of a new arrival trying to understand their new home. Maria was smart in recognizing things quickly.

A stocky lady with a cheerful face came over to greet them. 'Now, Maria, this is Madam Simone and she is in charge of the kitchens and the dining hall. She will look after you now until you are assigned your room. She will take good care of you – she always does.'

Madam Simone gave Madam Tibia a knowing smile and looked down at Maria.

'Come with me, my little dear, and I'll give you something warm to put in your stomach.' The two walked away together.

Madam Tibia turned and saw the tall, strong figure of Madam Beatrice standing in the doorway, carrying her stock folder under her arm. *Yes, she's about the same height as Madam Celia,* thought Tibia as she gave Beatrice a nod.

Tibia returned to the large stone staircase that would take her back to the private quarters of La Madre, and to her own office next door. As she stepped onto her corridor Madam Tibia looked across at the door to the library. She couldn't resist a little peak inside. She opened the door quietly and popped her head around into the room. She smiled to herself as she saw a small, delicate figure putting books upon the shelf without even reading the catalogue number.

As it has always been, so it shall always continue to be, thought Madam Tibia to herself, and closed the door. She loved being at the Azafran Home for Girls. Most of all, she loved being close to La Madre; her dearest of friends. Still, there was much work to do.

La Madre sat back in her comfortable upholstered chair. Yes, she had known it without a doubt. All her body told her that she was right. Maria would be the one, just as she herself had been all those many years before. Now she realized that her own La Madre must herself have known on that first meeting that she, as a young five-year-old girl, was to succeed her. How important it was to know from the beginning. This changes everything. And the white laced handkerchief would soon be tied around Maria's hair, so the Madams would know too. It is all about *preparation*…and the rest; well, that's the way of the saffron.

Kingsley L. Dennis, PhD, is a full-time writer and researcher. He is the author of several critically acclaimed books including *The Sacred Revival, The Phoenix Generation, New Consciousness for a New World, Struggle for Your Mind, After the Car,* and the celebrated *Dawn of the Akashic Age* (with Ervin Laszlo). Kingsley is the author of numerous articles on social futures, new technologies, digital culture and new media, and conscious evolution.

Kingsley also runs a self-publishing imprint called Beautiful Traitor Books (www.beautifultraitorbooks.com) and is now writing books for the children's market. His most recent book was called *Sophie's Search for No-Where* (June 2017). Kingsley is UK-born and currently lives in Andalusia, Spain. For more information, visit his website www.kingsleydennis.com

Naomi Hasegawa, born in The Netherlands of a Spanish and German mother and a Japanese father, has been an artist since she could hold a pencil. As an avid reader, she has been very grateful to have been given a chance to combine two of her passions. Being freelance artist and a student of Life, amongst other things, she loves a good challenge and a chance to learn, and likes to treat those opportunities as the lessons life has to teach.

You can find her on www.naomihasegawa.com